Forbidden Desires
A BDSM Erotic Romance
by
Reba Bale

Table of Contents

Copyright

---

1.   https://paperorpixels.com/

About This Book

Forbidden fruit tastes even sweeter the second time around...

I never expected to be a widow at thirty-five. I also never expected to be homeless and bankrupt, living in my childhood bedroom. And I really never expected that I'd be falling for my sister's ex-husband. Again.

Liam and I had one night of passion twelve years ago before going our separate ways. But now that we've found each other again, he wants more than one night. He wants forever.

I try to resist him, but Liam is the master of sensual teasing. It turns out that I have a kinky side too, and I can't help but submit to him.

But will my sister ever forgive us if she realizes that we betrayed her?

"Forbidden Desires" is a high heat, light BDSM, erotic romance with a happy ending. If you like sweet but dominant men, quirky characters, and a little bit of humor with your spankings, check out "Forbidden Desires" today.

Author's note: This was previously published as "Forbidden Romance" episodes 1-15 on serial apps.

Be sure to check out a free preview of "Spanking & Sprinkles" by Reba Bale, right after this story!

Dedication

This book is dedicated to everyone who fell in love with the wrong person, whether they turned out to be the right person or not. Sometimes forbidden fruit is the sweetest.

Join My Newsletter

Want a free book? Join my weekly newsletter and you'll receive a fun subscriber gift. I promise I will only email you when there are new releases, free books, or special sales you'll want to see.

Visit my newsletter sign-up[3] page to join today.

Chapter One

"I think that's the last of it."

I sent my sister a grateful look. "Thanks for your help, Paula, I don't know what I'd do without you."

"Pay someone to help you move," she joked.

The truth was, I didn't have much to move. Just a few boxes of mementos, several suitcases full of clothes, and my precious laptop. It had been my lifeline the last two years as I'd done my penance and watched my husband waste away, ravaged by a disease that took him far too young.

Now that he was gone, I knew I was supposed to be grieving the loss of my husband, but honestly, all I felt was relief. Only a few people knew that I'd told him I wanted a divorce the day before his diagnosis.

I'd loved him once – or at least that's what I'd convinced myself. I supposed he'd loved me too, but eventually our relationship had devolved into fighting and hurt feelings and lies. When I found out about his pregnant girlfriend, I told Daniel I wanted out.

The next day I found him on the kitchen floor having a seizure. Thousands of dollars of testing later, they told him he had some kind of fatal neurological disease. They gave him two years to live. He'd beaten the odds, hanging on for three. At the end, I'd had to put him into a care facility, selling off almost everything we owned to pay for it. Even with employer-sponsored health insurance, long-term care was catastrophically expensive.

His last 'fuck you' was hanging on that long. He didn't even have the decency to die before I lost the house. His girlfriend didn't even have the decency to tell him about the abortion before she fled town, leaving me as the only one who could take care of him.

Now here I was, a thirty-five year old widow who was bankrupt, homeless, and God help me, moving back in with my parents.

I didn't need to wonder what I'd done to deserve such terrible karma. I already knew. Before I met my husband, I'd fallen in love with the wrong man. Liam had been engaged at the time, but I thought maybe he'd leave his fiancé for me. After all, he'd claimed to love me as much as I loved him.

We'd slept together just once. It had been the best night of my life.

Then he'd gone back to my sister, full of guilt and remorse. We'd never told her what happened, but as I slowly lost everything taking care of my unfaithful husband, I knew.

This was my punishment.

Liam had gone through with the wedding, but he and Paula had only made it five years. She'd fallen in love with someone else and although she swore that she never cheated on her husband, I suspected she had.

But who was I to judge?

I'd mostly avoided family events while they were married, always nervous that Liam or I would somehow give something away. Even now, looking at my sister filled me with enough guilt to make me feel nauseous.

"You ready to go?"

"Sure." I mustered up a small smile for my sister and followed her out to her SUV.

"Oh, did you hear the news?" Paula asked as she backed out of my driveway.

I tore my gaze away from the home I'd been so proud to buy, the one that belonged to the bank now.

"What news?"

"Liam is moving back to town."

I stiffened. Posen was a small town. If Liam was living there, there was no way I wouldn't run into him.

"Yeah, believe it or not, he's going into practice with Dad."

"What?"

My sister's head whipped around at my high-pitched tone.

"You know how close those two always were, and Dad helped him study for the bar. With Mom bugging him to scale back on work and start planning for retirement, he figured he'd better come up with a plan. Liam is buying him out so he can keep the practice in the family."

Our father owned the only law firm in town. He'd been practicing there for fifty years now. It made sense that he was ready to retire. But handing it over to his daughter's ex-husband? That seemed weird.

"Liam's not family," I reminded her. "Not anymore."

"Liam is the son Dad never had," Paula answered. "It's a good thing we stayed friends after the divorce because I'm pretty sure if he was forced to choose, Dad would have kept Liam not me."

Six hours later I lay in the bed in my childhood bedroom, staring at the ceiling. There were still stars stuck up there, the kind that glowed in the dark, but they'd long since lost whatever it was that made them shine.

It was an appropriate metaphor for my life.

I sat up with a sigh when I heard a knock on the door.

"Come in, Mom."

She'd been hovering around ever since I'd gotten here. I'd finally told her that I wanted to take a nap before dinner just so I could get a moment of peace. I knew she meant well, but both of my parents seemed to think I was perpetually seventeen instead of a grown-ass woman. I was waiting for them to give me a curfew to abide by while I stayed here.

"It's not Mom."

Fuck. I'd recognize that deep voice anywhere.

I hadn't seen Liam in twelve years, not since his wedding to my sister. My eyes quickly cataloged any changes. He had tiny lines at the corners of his eyes and bracketing his strong mouth, but that was the only sign he'd aged in all this time.

He wasn't super tall, maybe five ten or five eleven, and even though I knew that he was thirty-six now, he still was super fit with broad shoulders, strong biceps, a trim waist, and thick thighs.

I felt a rush of heat between my legs, confirming that my traitorous body was just as attracted to him as it had always been.

"Liam."

God, why was my voice so breathy?

"What are you doing here?"

"Can I come in?"

I nodded, and he pushed the door closed behind him, grabbing the chair from the desk and bringing it closer to the bed. He straddled the chair, giving me a searching look.

"Your mother invited me over for dinner. Given that we hadn't seen each other since the wedding, I thought maybe we should talk."

I'd gone to him before the ceremony, begging him not to marry my sister, not after what had happened between us, but he'd been resolved to honor his commitment. I'd scarcely made it through the wedding without bursting into tears. As soon as they'd cut the cake and tossed the bouquet I'd snuck out of the reception and started packing. I moved to the city shortly after that.

"There's really nothing to talk about."

He studied me with those warm brown eyes that were the exact same color as my secret addiction: Hershey's Kisses.

"I just...I don't want things to be awkward. My relationship with Paula, my partnership with your dad, things between could get complicated fast."

I stood up, brushing non-existent wrinkles from my jeans, and gave him a smile that he was smart enough to know was fake.

"There's nothing to worry about Liam. I'm only here temporarily, until I can get back on my feet."

"I'm sorry about your husband."

I raised one eyebrow. "Are you?"

He shook his head. "Not really. I hated the guy."

"You never even met him."

"Yeah, but he took something that I wanted. That really made me hate him."

"Something you wanted?" I asked in confusion.

He nodded, holding my gaze long enough to make me want to squirm.

"Yeah. You."

Chapter Two

"Let me get this straight, you're mad at my dead husband because you think he took me from you?"

Liam nodded.

"The same husband who married me while you were with my sister?" I clarified.

He nodded again. "It's why I made an excuse to skip your wedding."

I'd always assumed he'd skipped my wedding to avoid causing me stress. God knows *his* wedding had damn near killed me. I'd been grateful to him for skipping mine a couple of years later, even if we'd never talked about it.

"Have you had a head injury since I last saw you?" I finally asked.

One corner of his mouth moved up in a smirk that I remembered well. And damned if it didn't make my long-dormant nether regions flutter to life.

"No head injury." He leaned forward in his chair, enough that I could get a whiff of his cologne or shampoo, something pine scented.

"I realized I was making a terrible mistake when I was standing at the altar with Paula, but it was too late to pull back. I convinced myself that I'd give it a couple of years, that I owed it to your sister to try to make our marriage work. By the time I realized it was futile, you were already married. But that doesn't mean I stopped thinking about you."

I leaped off my bed so quickly that I got a head rush. I moved around the twin-sized mattress, putting it between us as a barrier.

"You don't get to say that Liam. It's not fair."

He pushed to standing, walking around the bed with an intense look in his eyes. For a moment I felt like a gazelle being stalked by a lion. I resisted the urge to step back, instead standing my ground. I wasn't a pushover. I hadn't been back then, and I certainly wasn't now.

He stopped six inches away from me, which forced me to tilt my head up to look at him. That really pissed me off. I arched one eyebrow, waiting for him to speak.

"I'm sorry, Coco," he said, using the nickname he'd given me back when he first started my sister.

"For what?"

He huffed out a deep sigh.

"For marrying your sister when I knew it was wrong, for sleeping with you, for standing by while you married a man you didn't love."

My heart sped up in my chest.

"I loved him."

God, I didn't even sound convincing to my own ears.

"At least I thought I did when we got married."

"And after?"

"It was complicated."

"Paula said he was an asshole towards you."

I was surprised by this news. I'd never talked to my sister – or anyone else in my family – about the issues in my marriage. "How did she—?"

"Your sister is more perceptive than people give her credit for," he said.

He took the tiniest step closer, until a little more than an inch separated us.

"Liam."

"Coco."

Our eyes met and held, and it was like being held by a tractor beam. I couldn't look away. He lifted one hand slowly, giving me time to pull away, and despite my brain screaming at me to do just that, I couldn't.

Liam curved his palm against my cheek, and I was immediately brought back to the last time I saw him.

***

"What are you doing here, Coco? It's almost time for the ceremony to start."

"Are you really going through with it?" I whispered. "You're going to stand up there and marry my sister after what happened between us?"

"It was a mistake, you know that. It never should have happened."

"Which part? The one where you ordered me to suck your cock? Or the part where you made me come three times and then held me all night?"

Liam winced.

"It was wrong."

"You think I don't know that?" I asked angrily. "You think I like knowing how it would hurt Paula if she found out? But I can't...I couldn't..."

I stopped to wipe away the tears that were falling down my cheek, no doubt ruining my carefully applied make-up.

"I thought...you said you love me."

He lifted one hand to cup my cheek, his thumb wiping away a stray tear.

"I do love you, but I made a commitment to your sister. What we feel right now, it's wrong. It's not real."

"It feels real," I sniffled.

"We'll just have to get over it."

***

I shifted away until Liam's hand dropped from my cheek.

"You should go Liam."

"Kids! Dinner's ready!"

My mother's voice came from the bottom of the stairs, clear as day despite my bedroom door being closed. Mom always did have a voice that carried.

"Coming!" I yelled back.

Liam grabbed my wrist as I moved around him, stopping me in my tracks. I ignored the little zings that shot up my arm from his touch.

"I've waited a long time for this Coco."

I stared at the floor. "What?"

"For us both to be single at the same time."

I whipped around to face him, breaking his hold on my wrist, irritation rolling through me. What did he think? That I was easy pickings now that my husband had died? That with me coming home with my tail tucked between my legs, broke and homeless, I'd be grateful for any crumbs of his attention?

"Nothing's going to happen Liam. Maybe you think I'm needy and pathetic and vulnerable right now..."

"I don't think that all."

"Then I don't understand, what you think is happening here?"

"I came up to say hello to an old friend, and to clear the air between us," he said. "But the minute I laid eyes on you, I realized that I was still in love with you."

I was shaking my head before he even finished. "You are not still in love with me. We haven't even seen each other in twelve years!"

He moved closer, and this time I gave in to the impulse and stepped backward. He followed. Another two steps and my back hit the dresser against the wall. Liam wasn't tall, but he was broad – he'd filled out and bulked up in the years since I'd last seen him – and when he placed his hands on the dresser on either side of my shoulders, I felt completely surrounded by him.

My nipples hardened against the thin fabric of my shirt, traitors that they were.

Liam lowered his head, placing a kiss on the top of my shoulders. When I didn't knee him in the balls, he kissed his way up to the juncture of my neck, gently sucking my skin into his mouth.

Was it possible to come from neck play? If so, I was already halfway there. And for a woman who hadn't had an orgasm that wasn't self-induced in over five years, that was saying a lot.

"Don't you dare mark me," I breathed.

He released my skin, kissing his way up my neck, my jaw, and finally to the shell of my ear while I just stood there, head bent to the side, completely unable to push him away.

For the briefest instant, he slid his tongue around the edges of my ear before whispering the words that I knew I'd be analyzing for the rest of the night.

"You're mine Coco. It's only a matter of time before I'm inside you again, and this time, when I do, I'm never letting you go."

Chapter Three

"Hey Dad, do you have a minute?"

My father looked up from his giant oak desk, a smile curving his lips. "Of course sweetheart, come on in."

I stepped inside the familiar office where Paula and I had visited him a million times growing up and dropped into one of the visitor chairs.

"I'm sorry to ask you this when you're already doing so much for me right now, but I've got a problem."

Dad waved his hand dismissively. "You're our daughter, we don't mind helping you out until you get back on your feet."

"It's about Mom. I don't think she completely understands what it means that I work at home. She interrupts me several times a day, even when I remind her that I'm working. This morning she was vacuuming the hallway right outside my room when I was on a call, then on that same call she burst into my room asking if I had any dirty underwear to add to a load of delicates she was putting into the washing machine."

I heard a chuckle behind me and whipped around in my chair to see Liam standing in the doorway.

"Eavesdropping is not polite."

He smirked. "I came in to see if Ed wanted to go to lunch and I couldn't help but overhear your dilemma."

His gaze shifted to my father. "Why don't we let her use April's old office?" he suggested. "It's empty anyway."

"Oh no, I didn't come here looking for a handout, just advice for talking to my mother. She doesn't seem to understand that my working at home still means I have set work hours and tasks to focus on."

"Liam's right honey, you should use the office. It'll be quieter and the internet is better here anyway."

"Are you sure? I can pay you a little bit for rent..."

"It's open space Colleen," my father told me. "If we need it back we'll kick you out, don't worry."

"In that case, thank you. I really appreciate it." I stood up to leave. "I'll bring my stuff in tomorrow."

"You should come to lunch with us."

Liam's words sounded like a suggestion, but his tone sounded like an order. It made me bristle.

"You kids go on ahead," Dad said, already turning back to his computer. "I need to finish this filing. But bring me back something please, Liam."

"You got it."

I followed Liam out of the office, his hand burning against my lower back like a brand. As soon as we cleared the door, I stepped away from him.

"I don't really have time for lunch."

"Liar."

I slammed my hands on my hips. "Excuse me?"

"You're just afraid to be alone with me."

"I am not."

His eyes moved over my shoulders to the open door to my father's office.

"Do you really want to talk about this here?"

"No."

"Then let's talk over lunch."

I hadn't seen him since he'd come up to my bedroom a few nights ago. I'd endured a torturously long dinner with him and my parents, his eyes pinned to me almost the entire time, the fire in them reminding me of the way he'd kissed his way up my neck. I'd been so hot and bothered I could scarcely concentrate on dinner.

I'd half expected him to contact me but when he didn't, it just confirmed my suspicion that he was playing with me. Well, two could play.

"Fine, we'll have lunch but you're buying."

"Wouldn't have it any other way," he said smoothly.

We exited the office and walked up the street to a little café that had opened since I'd moved away. Daisy's was a cute place, light and airy, with small tables covered with starched white tablecloths decorated with a daisy design. The small flowers gave the tables a hint of whimsy.

The hostess led us to a table in the far corner. I slid into a seat against one wall, expecting Liam to sit across from me, but instead he sat to the side.

"What's good here?" I asked, scanning the menu.

"Everything is delicious," he said, but when I looked up his gaze was on me, not the menu.

"Stop it," I whisper shouted, cognizant of the way gossip traveled like wildfire in small towns.

"Stop what?"

"Stop staring at me like you want to bend me over the table and fuck me."

"I don't want to bend you over the table."

I shot him a skeptical look.

"I want to see your face when you come. Your expression is quite beautiful."

I kicked him in the shins. "We are never talking about that again."

Any response he was planning was interrupted by the waitress. We ordered our food, placing an order for my father, then watched the waitress walk away. I hadn't seen him move, but somehow Liam was closer to me now, his knee pressing against mine.

"Go out with me tonight."

I glanced around the café, looking for any familiar faces.

"No. We are not dating. Or doing anything else."

I jumped as I felt a hand land on my thigh. It inched upward, taking my skirt with it. My entire body felt instantly electrified.

"What are you doing?" I asked, completely irritated by how breathless my voice sounded.

Liam didn't answer. He continued moving upward, until his pinky finger met the elastic at the bottom of my panties. His fingers shifted around, going for my center, and I slammed my thighs together, trapping his fingers between them.

Another smirk.

He leaned closer, until I could feel his breath moving against the sensitive skin of my ear.

"Open your legs."

My eyes snapped to his at the dark command in his tone. I'd never heard him talk like that. In the blink of an eye, easy-going Liam was gone, leaving someone more commanding in his place. My body obeyed before my mind caught up with the change.

"Good girl," he whispered into my ear.

His fingers slid across the fabric of my panties a few times before sliding beneath to find my center. My breath caught. Somehow I was already growing aroused, as if he'd pressed some kind of long-dormant 'on' button for my libido.

Liam rubbed back and forth a few times before slipping between my pussy lips, finger going right to my clit. I gasped as he circled the little nub with the pad of one finger.

"Be quiet," he whispered. "Someone might hear you."

I shivered, and the smirk was back.

"You like the idea of being caught."

"I don't."

My voice was weak, as if even my own mouth didn't believe the lie.

"Yet you flooded my fingers with cream when I mentioned it."

God help me, I did.

"You're a naughty girl."

He kept circling my clit, around and around, gradually adding pressure. My hips began moving to meet him and I said a silent prayer of gratitude that the long tablecloth would hide what was happening here.

Pressure was building deep inside me, yet I needed more.

"Liam," I whispered.

Clearly he heard the plea in my voice because he shifted his hand until he could slide one long finger into my channel. My muscles clenched against him, and he started thrusting it slowly inside of me.

My fingers gripped the edge of the table, turning white with the effort of holding myself still when all I wanted to do was hump his hand and cry out in ecstasy. It had been a long time – so long – since I'd felt this way.

The fact that this was my sister's ex-husband who was also my father's business partner didn't seem to matter right now. The fact that we were in public didn't matter either. Not when my greedy pussy was desperate to be filled.

As if he heard my thoughts, Liam added a second finger, stretching my channel.

I closed my eyes, trying to breathe, as his skillful fingers brought me closer and closer to the relief I craved.

"Liam," I whispered, my voice needy.

"Go out with me tonight."

I turned my head, my thoughts jumbled as his words registered. "What?"

The fingers inside me picked speed, moving in and out quickly.

"Go out with me tonight, Coco," he repeated. "I'll give you what you need."

He pressed his thumb against my little button and my body started to tremble. The first tremors of an orgasm were building deep inside me.

"No. I can't."

I nearly cried out as his fingers immediately left my body. Liam unfolded his napkin and calmly wiped my arousal off of his skin.

"Wha—why'd you stop?"

"You want more, Coco? You know where to find me."

Just then the waitress came up to our table, carrying our plates as well as well as the to-go bag with my father's lunch.

"I'll take a box for mine too, please," he told her. "I need to get back to the office."

As Liam strode away without so much as a backward glance, I ignored my throbbing pussy and tried to figure out what had just happened.

Chapter Four

"Do you know if we still have the death penalty in this state?"

My friend Mya raised her eyebrows in surprise. We'd recently reconnected after I'd lost everything and moved back to my hometown, picking up right where we'd left off as if it hadn't been over a dozen years since we'd been friends. I was glad, I really needed a friend at this point in my life.

Just like when we were teenagers, the two of us were holed up in my childhood bedroom talking and laughing. Unlike when we were teenagers, we were passing a bottle of tequila between us.

Mya was married with two kids so we couldn't drink in peace at her house. Since I was homeless and bankrupt, I was staying with my parents temporarily. Hopefully temporarily.

"Girls?" My mother tapped on the door and instinctively I hid the bottle of booze behind the table, as if we were in trouble. "Do you want a snack?"

My mother was under the impression I was still a kid, not a grown woman.

"No Mom, we're good thanks."

"Actually, I wouldn't mind a snack," Mya whispered.

I opened a drawer and tossed her a canister of Pringles. "Here you go."

"Why do you want to know about the death penalty?" she asked.

"You have to promise to keep this just between us."

She leaned forward with an eager look.

"I promise."

I gave her a hard stare. "You can't tell Steve," I said, referring to her husband. "Or anyone else ever, even if they torture you."

She rolled her eyes. "I'm not one of those women who has to tell her husband everything," she scoffed. "We've been married way too long for that."

I leaned closer.

"My mom was driving me crazy, always interrupting me while I'm working, so my dad offered me to let me use an empty office at the law firm."

Mya nodded and made a 'go on' gesture.

"Which means I'm around Liam every day."

"I thought you liked your brother-in-law," she said. "I always thought you had a crush on him when we were younger."

"Ex brother-in-law," I reminded her. "And I did like him. Turns out, it wasn't solely one-sided."

Her eyes widened. "But your sister..."

"She never knew. I'm ashamed to tell you this, but one night before they got married, things got a little out of hand."

"Out of hand like you fooled around, or out of hand like you did the horizontal mambo?"

"We fucked like bunnies all night," I confided. "Then I told him that I loved him, and he said he felt the same."

She clapped a hand over her mouth.

"The day after I...well, I begged him to leave my sister. He refused and went through with the wedding."

"Oh my God!"

"I know, it was a shitty thing to do. I was much younger then of course, but it's no excuse. You know how it is when you're a slave to your hormones."

"Oh yeah."

It felt good to finally tell someone what happened, after keeping it a secret all these years. I'd never once regretted that Liam had the cooler head that day. If he'd made a different choice, we would have devastated my sister.

"The night I got back into town, he came here and told me he'd made a mistake back then. He says he wants us to give it another chance."

Mya made a squeaking sound from behind her palm.

"Of course I said no. I mean, how Jerry Springer can this situation get? My sister's ex-husband and father's friend and law partner who I slept with once years ago says he's still in love with me? It's crazy."

"He's in love with you?"

"So he says. But there's more."

Mya cracked open the can of Pringles and grabbed a handful, shoving chips into her mouth like it was popcorn.

"Do tell."

"He kissed me."

"How was it? You have to tell me, I'm an old married woman, I haven't had anyone new kiss me in fifteen years."

I sighed. "Incredible."

I took a long swallow of tequila and then passed the bottle back to my friend.

"What's the problem? You're both single."

"If you and Steve got divorced, would you want one of your sisters to date him?"

"Oh. Well. No."

"Besides, my husband just died."

"You didn't love him," she reminded me. "He was a cheating asshole."

I'd told her the whole story last time we hung out.

"Yeah, but how does it look if I'm dating someone before he's even cold in his grave?"

"First of all, he was cremated. Secondly, this isn't Victorian England. We don't have all those societal expectations about mourning periods."

I shook my head. "It's too weird."

"What does all this have to do with the death penalty?"

"Oh yeah well, Liam is torturing me now, trying to get me to break down."

"Torturing you how?"

"He keeps getting me, um, excited, and then walking away. "

"He's edging you?"

"Kind of. He...," I lowered my voice again, "fingered me in a restaurant the other day, then stopped before I finished. Every time I see him in the office, he slides his hand against mine or rubs his hip against my ass, like it's just an innocent touch but then he looks at me with this fire in my eyes and I know it's no accident."

Mya rolled her lips in, like she was trying to keep from laughing.

"And then there was an incident today in the copy room..."

***

I walked into the copy room to scan a document, and Liam was in there looking for office supplies. His chocolate brown eyes darkened with pleasure.

"Fancy meeting you here."

"I just need to scan something."

I tried to walk around him, but he blocked my path, somehow maneuvering me behind the open door, my back pressed against the wall.

"What are you doing? We're at work."

He lowered his head to lick the side of my neck. "So?"

"Anyone could see us."

He shifted to meet my gaze. "As I recall, that hits a kink for you."

"I'm not kinky."

One brown eyebrow raised almost to his hairline.

"Really Coco? You think you're not kinky?"

"I'm as vanilla as they come," I said breathily.

Quicker than I could process, he pulled my hands over my head, capturing both of my wrists in one of his strong hands. The paper I'd come to scan drifted toward the floor.

"So if I restrain you, even a little, it's not exciting for you? Not at all?"

"No."

Even I wasn't convinced by my response.

His other hand landed on my stomach, slowly moving downward. I sent up a little prayer of thanks that I was wearing thick pants today to ward off the cold. He wouldn't be able to feel how wet I was through the fabric.

The sound of my zipper filled the room, and I pulled against his hand as I realized his intention. He held me tight as his fingers slipped lower.

"Stop!"

His fingers immediately stilled, half in and half out of my panties.

When I didn't say anything else, he leaned in until our lips were only an inch apart.

"Let me make you feel good, Coco."

Because I was a weak, weak woman, a woman who hadn't had sex in more years than I could count, I nodded.

His lips crashed against mine as his fingers dipped into my panties, sliding between my lower lips. He made a sound of masculine pleasure as he encountered the evidence of my arousal. His fingers slid back and forth in my channel, increasing my excitement, as his tongue explored my mouth.

With my hands still immobilized over my head, I was trapped. And God help me, I loved it.

I lifted one leg, intending to wrap it around him, but paused when Liam removed his fingers from my pussy and landed a sharp slap to my hip. It surprised me more than it hurt.

"Don't move, I'm in control."

Had his voice ever been this deep? He chuckled darkly as his fingers returned to my pussy just as a rush of moisture flooded my core. He cupped my mound, giving it a squeeze that was just short of painful.

"Go out with me," he whispered as he started fucking me with his fingers again.

I ground against his hand, so close to the release I needed. His fingers stilled, and I let out a little whine. The hand shackling my wrists tightened.

"Go out with me, Coco."

I hesitated, waging a silent battle in my head until common sense won out.

"I can't."

Liam gave me a long stare, and I sighed in relief as he began fucking me with his fingers again. I rolled my hips, trying to get the pressure I needed to get over the edge. I was so close...

Without warning, he removed his fingers again, pressing one against my lips. Dutifully I opened for him, sucking my essence off the rough skin of his fingers. Then he stepped back, releasing my hands.

"What—-?"

"You know where to find me when you're ready."

He stalked out of the copy room, leaving me half naked. My breath hitched as I brushed against my throbbing clit, pulling my panties back into place.

"I'm going to kill that bastard!"

***

When I finished my story, Mya was staring at me with a mixture of wonder, amusement, and jealousy.

"God DAMN girl, that's so hot! You've got to hit that!"

I shook my head.

"He wants to date. He wants forever. I'm not a forever girl. Not anymore."

Chapter Five

"You're working late."

I looked up to see Liam in the doorway of my office. I'd successfully avoided seeing him the last two days, mostly because he'd been in court, and I hadn't expected to see him back here again today.

"Just taking advantage of the quiet," I said neutrally.

After losing everything when my husband died, I was picking up some freelance clients to generate extra income. My day job paid well, but I was still paying off medical bills and other expenses from my husband's death. I thought, not for the first time, that I should have just divorced him when I found out about his affair. Instead, I'd stayed by his side through his long and expensive slide into death, thinking maybe it was my penance for betraying my sister all those years ago.

And the cause of that betrayal was staring at me from the doorway, looking all kinds of sexy with his tie loosened and his hair mussed, as if he'd been running his fingers through his thick brown locks.

The sooner I got out of debt, the sooner I could get my own place again and be free of my oversolicitous mother and the ex-brother-in-law who was waging a campaign of seduction against me.

Liam stepped closer, his eyes skimming my face.

"You look tired, Coco."

"I'm fine."

Or I would be when I no longer had to sleep in the tiny twin bed in my childhood bedroom.

"How about dinner?"

I shook my head.

"I have some stuff to finish then I've got to get home. See you later."

I turned my attention back to my computer, but instead of leaving, he dropped into one of the chairs across from my desk.

"Was there anything else?" I asked impatiently.

"Yeah, how long are you going to keep pretending that there's nothing between us?"

"As long as it takes for you to get the message that there's nothing between us," I snipped.

One brown eyebrow rose skeptically.

"I bet you got wet the instant you saw me in the doorway."

Damn it, how did he know?

"Not true," I lied.

He stalked around my desk, trapping me between his body and the sides of my L-shaped desk. He dropped to his knees in front of me, one hand on each arm of my chair.

"Liam," I said sternly. "I don't have time for this."

My eyes met his defiantly. I don't know what he saw in my gaze, but one corner of his mouth quirked up.

"I think the lady doth protest too much," he whispered.

"Was there something not clear about me saying that I want you to leave me the fuck alone?" I snapped.

"You say that, yet every time I touch you it ends up with you humping my hand."

"You're disgusting."

His hands moved to my thighs, pulling them apart so he could squeeze in between them. Damned if I didn't let him.

What was it about this man? All he had to do was touch me and every bit of common sense flew out of my head. He wasn't lying about the me humping his hand part.

"Here's the thing Coco, if I really thought you weren't interested, I would leave you alone, despite my feelings for you."

His hand moved down to cup my mound and I knew he could feel the heat there, maybe even some of the dampness seeping through.

"But I can see the truth in your eyes, and I can feel the truth here," he squeezed my mound. "You want me."

A soft moan escaped me despite my best efforts. This man had me wound so tight I couldn't think of anything besides how much I wanted him to fuck me.

"I want to be able to eat nothing but Hershey's kisses for dinner too, but that doesn't mean I do it."

Those eyes that reminded me of my favorite treat crinkled at the corners.

"Life has dealt you a hard time these last few years," he reminded me with soft sympathy. "Maybe you should let yourself have a treat."

Suddenly he spun my chair around, pulling my wrists behind me. Before I realized what was happening, I felt something silky wrap around my wrists, immobilizing me. His tie.

"What are you doing?"

I pulled against my restraints, but that moment of hesitation had been all that Liam needed to secure my wrists behind my chair. I should have been angry. Maybe a little scared. Instead I was...turned on.

Liam turned my chair back again, so I was facing him.

"I love the way that position puts your tits on display for me," he said.

I looked down to see my breasts pulling against the thin fabric of my shirt, the hard points of my nipples visibly pressing through and betraying me.

"It's cold in here," I said, but my tone didn't convince either of us.

He pinched one nipple between his fingers, and even through the fabric of my shirt and bra I could feel his touch searing me like a brand.

"I'll make you a deal."

"What?"

"If I make you come in less than five minutes, you'll agree to go out with me on a real date."

"Five minutes?" I scoffed. "That's nothing."

His eyes flared in challenge.

"Four?" he negotiated.

"Let's see if you can do it in three, hotshot."

Wait, what was I agreeing to? The man could practically make me come with just a smoldering look, kind of like the one he was sending me right now.

"Okay, but time starts after I get you out of these pants." His hands went to the waistband of my boring khaki pants. "It's only fair."

"Wait."

He stopped immediately, his eyes going to mine.

"Close the door."

He smirked. "Oh no, we both know it's more fun if you're afraid someone will catch us."

I pressed my knees against his ribs as hard as I could, making him wince.

"Close the door," I said firmly.

"Fine, but once that door is closed, I'm in charge."

I shouldn't have liked that as much as I did. But after all these years of managing everything in my marriage, managing my husband's care as his illness progressed, juggling work and home and having everything – every single thing – be my responsibility for so long, the idea that I could, just this once, let go and let someone else be in charge was incredibly appealing.

Liam crossed the room and closed the door, the sound of the lock engaging loud in the silent space. He was back in front of me in seconds, making quick work of opening my pants and sliding them down my legs. He tossed my khakis onto my desk, then removed my panties, shoving them into the front pocket of his suit pants.

"Hey!"

"Souvenir," he said cheekily. "You'll get them back if you win. Wait, what am I saying, you're going to win, just not the way you think you are."

"Good God you've turned into an arrogant asshole over the years."

"You have no idea."

He scooted closer, his eyes studying my bare pussy until I was squirming in my chair, moisture leaking from between my lower lips. I was so desperate for him right now there was a good chance that he was going to win the bet without touching me.

Liam made a big show of setting the timer on his phone.

"Ready?" he asked.

When I nodded, he hit the start button, whipped my legs over his shoulders, and dove right in. His tongue was rough and aggressive as it slid inside my slit, exploring my folds.

I was in a weird position with my hands tied behind my back and my legs over his shoulders, the combination making me almost immobile. Liam's hands gripped my hips hard enough to bruise, and he sucked a section of my labia into his mouth, biting down softly and making me moan. He nipped up and down both of my lower lips before diving between them, licking me roughly from end to end.

He glanced up from between my legs and sent me a wicked smile.

"You're so fucking wet for me, and you taste delicious."

Before I could respond, he thrust his tongue into my channel and started pumping in and out while his fingers circled the area around my clit. I rolled my hips up to meet him, desperate to get more pressure where I needed it most. But despite the time limit, he continued to tease me, driving up my arousal until I was ready to scream.

He continued eating me out while sliding one hand up underneath my shirt, moving up the soft swell of my stomach until he was able to cup one breast. He somehow managed to shift my bra cup down enough to pinch my bare nipple between his fingers.

"Oh my God, Liam."

My entire body was on fire, and I was fighting the urge to come, torn between wanting to win the bet and wanting to finally, finally get some relief.

He removed his tongue long enough to bite out, "Let go, Coco. Come for me. Now!"

Then the fingers of one hand pinched my clit at the exact same time as the other hand pinched my nipple, and I lost completely it. My mind cleared of everything besides the waves of pleasure coursing through my body.

I pulled against my restraints, my back arching against the chair as I pushed my breast in his hand and ground my pussy against his face. I was beyond shame, beyond reason, moaning like a porn star as I took my pleasure in Liam's hands and mouth.

He didn't pause, continuing to stroke and lick and touch me as little tremors shook my body, extending my orgasm longer than I thought possible.

Suddenly a loud noise sounded, drowning out my moans and sighs. Liam looked up and gave me a look so intense I shivered.

"Time's up."

I damn near cried as he pulled away, leaving my dripping pussy on display as he turned off the timer on his phone.

"You look beautiful tied up and debauched," he said darkly, his words making me shiver. "I can't wait to tie you to my bed and bite every inch of your body."

God help me but I damn near came again from that little visual.

He spun me around, making quick work of untying my hands, then leaned over my chair and gave me a kiss that was hard and possessive and left me breathless.

"I'll pick you up tomorrow after work. You might want to bring an overnight bag."

I opened my mouth to protest but couldn't do anything more than sigh as he landed a light tap on my throbbing clit and then strode across the room, leaving me feeling almost bereft.

"See you tomorrow for our date."

Chapter Six

"This is stupid, right?"

I was holed up in the handicapped stall in the ladies' room talking to my friend Mya about my upcoming date with Liam. Fortunately, there were only two other women who worked in the office, and I knew for a fact one of them was in court and the other had just gone to lunch.

I could have talked to my friend in my office, but those walls were pretty thin and with my father's office right next door, I didn't want to take a chance on him overhearing me. I had no idea how my father would feel about me sleeping with his law practice partner – and the man who used to be married to his other daughter.

Today was not the day I wanted to find out.

"The man made you come in under three minutes," Mya reminded me. "You think you can do better than that?"

I sighed deeply. "It's more than that and you know it."

There was a long pause, and I knew even without seeing her that my friend was thinking about the best way to say something to me.

"Just say it," I told her.

"I think all your worry about what Paula might say, what your father might say, what anyone might say, it's all an excuse you're using to avoid the real issue."

"What real issue?" I asked, fully knowing the answer but stalling for time.

"You're still in love with him."

"No, I'm not," I protested weakly.

I totally was, but it scared the shit out of me.

"You loved him once and he rejected you, so now you don't want to trust him," Mya said. "Even though you and I both know he did the right thing by not leaving your sister at the altar."

"He totally did," I agreed. "Even though it didn't work out between them, at least my sister and he had a chance."

"And now you and Liam can have a chance."

"It's too late for us."

My friend sighed. "Colleen, it's not too late. It's time to stop punishing yourself for something that happened years ago. If Daniel dying in his thirties taught you anything, it should be that life is too short. You don't want to be on your deathbed wishing you'd fucked Liam again when you had the chance."

I laughed. "You really think that'll be my focus when I'm dying?"

"It will be if you don't at least give this thing a chance. What's the worst that can happen? You live happily ever after?"

"Actually, the worst that can happen is that my sister finds out what happened."

Mya sighed. "Maybe you should just tell her."

"What? After all this time?"

"If it's the thing that's going to stand between you and Liam being together, yes."

"I'm taking this to my grave Mya, and you promised you would too."

"My lips are sealed, don't worry. But give this Liam thing a chance. Open yourself up to the possibility that you can be happy with a man for the first time in your life."

"Okay, you're right Mya, thanks for talking me off the ledge."

"Any time. Now go have the kind of hot and energetic sex I remember fondly from before my kids were born."

An hour later I met Liam outside the office. He must not have had any court appearances today because he was dressed more casually in black slacks and a light blue shirt.

His eyes softened when he saw me walk towards him.

"Hey, you came."

I realized then he'd been worried.

"Yeah, but I need to be sure I get home tonight."

"Why?"

"The last thing I need to do is explain to my mother why I'm not in bed by curfew."

"She gave you a curfew?" he asked incredulously.

"No, but she probably would if she thought I had anything fun to do."

He threaded his fingers through mine and tugged me towards his car. "Oh, you have something fun to do. Me."

I rolled my eyes as I slid into the passenger seat of his Lexus. "Haha."

Liam backed out of his parking space and headed for the northwest side of town.

"Where are we going for our date?" I asked.

"My house."

I was immediately annoyed. "I thought this was a date, not a booty call."

"Can't it be both?" he smirked.

"Liam!"

He shot me a quick glance before returning his eyes to the road.

"I'm cooking you dinner, and we'll talk and then if you're a good girl I'll make you come a couple of times before I take you home to your parents."

"A couple of times? That's ambitious."

"Please, I made you come in under three minutes yesterday. How hard do think it's going to be when I have a few hours to work with?"

"There's no reason to brag."

"I saw your expression as you came all over my face. There's definitely a reason to brag."

We were mostly silent on the short drive to his house. Liam lived in a nice little craftsman at the dead end of a quiet street. It was the kind of house you'd buy to raise a family. I felt a pang of sadness that having a child wasn't in the cards for me.

I wondered if he and Paula had ever tried to get pregnant. If so, she'd never mentioned it to me. Although now that I have thought about it, my sister rarely mentioned Liam when they were married. I wondered why.

"Did you buy this place after the divorce?" I asked. "Or after you came back?"

"I just moved in like two months ago," he told me. "After I sold my condo in the city."

I knew that he'd moved back to become a partner in my father's law practice. Dad was gradually stepping down, wanting to retire with my mother.

His house was nicely restored with hardwood floors, stark white walls framed by detailed moldings, and beautiful built-in shelves and cabinets. He'd decorated it simply with comfortable furniture and a few art prints.

I stepped over to the mantle, checking out the photos he'd displayed there. There was one of him and my father fishing, each of them holding ridiculously large fish, and another one of him with his family at some event, my sister at his side. I studied the photo carefully. They looked happy, but I knew as well as anyone that appearances could be deceiving.

Liam came up behind me, wrapping his arm around my waist. Without thinking, I leaned into him. He pressed a quick kiss on my cheek, then nipped at the shell of my ear, making me shiver.

"Are you hungry?"

"Sure."

"Good. I prepped some food last night, it won't take long to cook it. Join me in the kitchen?"

"Yeah."

I followed him into the kitchen. It was bright and airy with white cabinets and plenty of workspace. I poured us some wine while Liam worked at the stove, searing some steaks under the broiler and heating up some kind of a potato dish that he'd prepped the night before.

"Do you want me to make a salad or something?" I asked, not used to watching anyone besides my mother work in the kitchen.

"Already have one in the fridge. Just needs dressing."

I wondered if Paula did the cooking when they were married.

"We took turns, since we both were working full-time," Liam said, making me realize that I'd spoken my question out loud.

"Paula never talked too much about you when you were married, I just realized that."

Liam turned to lean against the counter, his eyes turning wary. He hesitated for so long that I didn't think he was going to speak.

"It's because she suspected that we were more than friendly."

"What?" My question came out as a high-pitched shriek.

"We had a big fight about a year after we were married," he said. "Somehow you came up and I don't know what I said or what she thought she saw, but she accused me of having feelings for you. I, well, I couldn't deny it. I couldn't lie. And then she said, 'well maybe you married the wrong sister' and in the heat of the moment I told her I thought I had."

I collapsed onto a chair in shock.

"What happened then?"

"We separated for about a month, but then we got back together."

"I never heard a word about this."

"I don't think your parents knew about the separation, we kept it on the down low while we tried to figure out whether or not we wanted to stay together. In the end, we decided to go to couples counseling, which helped. And that was when you were getting serious about your dickhead husband. When you guys got engaged, I think that convinced Paula that I wasn't going to leave her for you."

"Oh my God, I can't believe she never mentioned this."

"That's why I think she's going to be fine when she hears that we're together now. She always figured we would be."

"We're not together now," I corrected him. "I agreed to one date. On a bet."

"Oh, we're together. I know you need time Coco, and I'm willing to go slow, but make no mistake, you and I are going to be together."

Chapter Seven

"Make no mistake, you and I are going to be together."

My heart pounded at Liam's words, but true to his word, he was going to give me some time. By unspoken agreement we downshifted into small talk, eating our dinner and updating each other about our lives. I'd missed Liam, missed the way we could just talk for hours, although I hadn't realized it before.

We'd been friends, he and I, before he'd started dating my sister. It had made it easy for the three of us to hang out together, at least until Liam and Paula had gone away to college. I was a year behind them in school and while they were off in the city having new adventures, I was stuck in high school without my two best friends.

By the time I'd gotten to college, they'd gone from casual dating to serious boyfriend and girlfriend. One night after too much tequila and a shared joint Paula had shared that she and Liam had lost their virginity together right before their high school graduation.

I hadn't had romantic feelings for him at the time, although I'd always thought he was hot. The feelings had only started later. I couldn't pinpoint when exactly but at some point, I'd gone from feeling friendly towards him to fantasizing about him. Loving him.

It wasn't until right before the wedding that I discovered that he'd had the same change in his emotions. It was two days before the wedding and Liam and I had spent most of the day together, running errands and finalizing things for the ceremony while Paula had a spa day with some of her friends.

We'd ended up at his house after we finished, ordering pizza and tying ribbons on those stupid little bags of almonds that people liked to hand out at weddings. After a few beers, Liam confessed that he had cold feet.

***

"I shouldn't be attracted to someone else when I'm getting married to your sister, right?" He looked tortured.

I reared back in surprise. I'd never seen Liam look like anything but the doting fiancé.

"Attraction for people is probably normal, you're engaged, not dead," I said mildly. "You love my sister, don't you?"

"I thought I did, but now I'm not sure."

"Why did you propose then?"

"She asked me to get married, and honestly I just went along with it."

I nodded. My sister could be pushy when she wanted something, and I knew that she'd wanted to lock Liam down for a while now.

He reached out and took my hand, his thumb stroking the skin on the back of my hand. His touch made my breath catch. We'd both stared at our hands for a long moment and then Liam was moving closer.

"What are you doing?" My voice had been breathless even as I leaned towards him.

"Testing a theory."

His lips had touched mine, tentatively at first, then more firmly. It was like my secret late-night fantasies were coming true, and I returned his kiss eagerly. Our hands were all over each other, testing and exploring, but when I felt his hand on my breast, I pulled back, common sense rearing its head.

"Wait. We shouldn't do this."

"I know."

He kissed me again. I'd never been kissed like this, so deeply, so passionately. When we broke apart the second time, I could see the bulge in his pants and feel the dampness between my thighs.

"I'm engaged to the wrong sister," he'd whispered against my lips. "You're the one I love. It's always been you."

"You're drunk. We're both drunk."

"I'm not so drunk that I don't know how I feel."

Then we kissed some more, and I ended up straddling his lap, dry humping him through our clothes.

"Tell me how you feel, Coco. Tell me that I'm crazy."

"You're not crazy," I said softly. "I've loved you forever. But I don't want to hurt my sister."

"I don't either," he said. "We'll go talk to her. Together. She'll understand."

And in the wee hours of the night, I'd believed that this was true. But when I woke up in his arms late the next morning, thoroughly debauched after we'd had sex more times than I could count, I had my doubts.

I wasn't the only one.

"What do we do now?" I'd whispered, afraid to break the sensual spell between us.

"Last night was the best night of my life, but I didn't plan for that to happen. I need some time to think," Liam told me. "If we're going to be together, I need to break up with Paula first, it's only right."

"If?"

My heart felt like it was breaking.

"I'm so confused, Coco. I made a commitment to your sister and I...well I care about her. I love her, but I'm not in love with her. But if I break up with her, it's going to kill her, and tear your family apart too."

"But you said you love me."

I don't think my voice had ever sounded this sad and pathetic.

"I do, and I know you love me too, but this all happened so fast. Let's spend some time apart and see how we feel tomorrow."

By the time we got to the rehearsal dinner later that day, Liam was full of regrets. Honestly, so was I. I couldn't see a solution to our problem. I could either be with Liam or be a good sister. I'd spent years chastising myself for choosing the first option.

Overcome with youthful emotions, I wasn't thinking clearly. Fortunately, Liam had been. And when he married my sister, I made a vow to never interfere with their relationship again.

***

"You're thinking awfully hard over there."

I looked up at Liam's words, realizing that I'd just been staring into space.

"I'm thinking about that night, and the decision we made – you made – afterward. It was the right one, I realize that, as much as I hated you for making it."

"I hated myself," he admitted. "Paula would have hated us both more if we'd made a different one. But that's all in the past now. We're getting our second chance, Coco."

"I just don't know if I can move past the guilt."

"Is that why you stayed with a guy who treated you like crap? Paying penance for your guilt?"

I looked up in surprise. Then again, Liam had always been incredibly astute.

"You know? I think you need to get out of your head." He got out of his chair and stalked towards me. "And I did promise you some orgasms."

"Liam, you can't fuck me into submission."

His eyes flared at the word submission, which reminded me of what had happened in my office.

"Do you tie a lot of women up?" I asked. "The way you did yesterday?"

He paused, as if choosing his words carefully.

"Over the years – after I broke up with your sister – I discovered that I like to be in control."

Something deep inside my core pulsed at his words.

"What does that mean exactly?"

"Sex is so much hotter with a little pain. A little torture."

"Torture?" My voice came out high and squeaky.

"Sensual torture," he clarified. "Edging. Tickling. Wax. Restraint. I'm not saying that I want to chain you to the wall and whip you, Coco, but I would like to handcuff you to my bed and tease you with a vibrator until you forget your own name."

Between my legs my panties had just disintegrated. My God, why was that so hot? I was strong and independent and yet, when Liam had tied me to a chair and immobilized my legs yesterday while he ate me out, I'd come harder than I had in my life.

"You like that."

I turned my head, refusing to meet his eyes. "Like what?"

He turned my chair to face him and leaned over me, sliding one long finger underneath my chin, forcing me to meet his hot gaze. It felt like he was looking right into my soul.

"You like the idea of me tying you down. Dominating you. Spanking you. Dripping hot wax all over your beautiful body until you're begging for my cock. Begging for my permission to come."

"I don't beg for anything," I snapped, but it was half-hearted.

"Wanna bet?"

Chapter Eight

Before I realized what was happening, Liam grabbed me by the waist and tossed me over his shoulder like a sack of potatoes.

"Hey!" I protested, pounding on his back. "We just ate. Put me down before I throw up on you!"

"You scarcely touched your dinner," he reminded me as he headed out of the kitchen. "And you haven't thrown up since grade school."

"You don't know that! Maybe I threw up while I was married."

I wiggled and kicked, trying to get free.

Thwack!

All the breath whooshed out of my body as Laim smacked my ass hard enough to sting.

"Hey!"

I wiggled some more and again his hand came down, harder this time.

Thwack!

"Be still," he ordered, his voice deeper than I'd ever heard it before. "Unless you want me to take you over my knee and make you behave."

I couldn't help the full body shiver those words elicited. And based on his dark chuckle, Liam felt it too.

Damn it, I was a strong, independent woman! I should not like being threatened with a spanking like a naughty child! When I began to struggle again Liam laughed.

"I knew you'd want a spanking."

We entered the bedroom and he pushed the door closed behind us. The world tilted again as he dropped me back to my feet. Liam's hands came up to cup my cheeks, holding my head in place as he crashed his lips against mine.

We'd kissed a couple of times since I'd gotten back but this kiss felt different. More dominant. More aggressive. More claiming. When he bit my lower lip, I opened willingly for him, my tongue meeting his in a battle for control. A battle I knew instinctively I would lose, but that didn't mean I wasn't going to try.

I was wearing a cute little wrap dress that I absolutely had not picked out just for my date for Liam, even though it was the most flattering outfit I owned. With one quick flick of his wrists, my ex-brother-in-law managed to untie the bow holding it together. He released my lips long enough to drag the dress off my shoulders and toss it to the floor, leaving me only in my matching navy blue bra and panties.

I hadn't picked those with him in mind either, and there was no way you'd get me to admit anything different.

Liam dominated my mouth, his hands sliding up and down my back, squeezing my ass, drawing me closer. I grabbed onto his waist, helpless to do anything but kiss him back. I'd forgotten why it was even a bad idea.

When he pulled back from me, my bra fell down my arms. I looked at it in confusion, never even noticing that he'd unhooked me. We both watched my breasts bounce free of their confinement.

When I stood only in my panties, Liam pulled me towards the bed. I thought he'd lay on top of me, or maybe even go down on me, but instead he sat down and pulled me face down over his lap.

"Wait, what are you doing?"

I tried to roll away, but one strong arm clamped down on my waist, holding me in place. Despite his actions, I knew that if I told him to, Liam would stop. I trusted him implicitly.

"I believe I promised you a spanking."

One large hand came down across the center of my ass, making me squeal.

"Hey, that hurts!"

Liam rubbed his hand over the seat of my underwear.

"I'm just warming you up, baby."

He landed a series of spanks, switching from one cheek to the other, each smack hard enough to sting even through the fabric of my panties. With each strike of his hand, I could feel my flesh compressing, then bouncing back as the heat spread.

After a few minutes I kind of relaxed into it, mesmerized by the steady rhythm of his hand. When he stopped, I couldn't help but sigh.

I felt a tug on the waistband of my panties, and then Liam slid my underwear around the globes of my ass and down to my knees.

"Wait. Stop."

Liam's hand stilled, resting on the back of my thighs.

"What are you doing?" I asked again.

"Now that I warmed you up, it's time for your real spanking."

I tried to wiggle away, but a sharp smack on my ass stopped my movement immediately.

"Okay, you proved your point, you can let me go now, Liam. This isn't funny."

I wished my voice sounded a little more convincing.

"It might not be funny, but it's definitely fun," he said, his voice teasing.

He slid my hand up my side until it touched his cock. He was rock hard. Reflexively, my fingers wrapped around his length. He hissed out a breath.

"You may be getting off on this, but I'm not," I said stubbornly.

I was lying, and of course he had to prove it to me by sliding his hand between my thighs and dipping one finger into my channel.

"You're awfully wet for someone who's not enjoying this," he teased.

Removing his finger, he brought it over my head and in front of my face.

"Taste how excited you are," he ordered, and when he pressed his finger against my lips, I couldn't help but open for him, swirling my tongue around his digit.

"Do you really want me to stop?" he asked as he pulled away.

I hesitated for a long moment, debating my options. The truth was, I was liking this way more than I thought I would, way more than I should probably, and I wanted to see what would happen next.

"No, don't stop. Not yet."

His hand returned to my ass, rubbing my skin for a moment before he began spanking me again. His hand moved up and down, side to side, covering every inch of my ass with sharp slaps. He kept a steady pace but varied the pressure, alternating between light taps and sharper smacks.

The longer it went on, the more the heat rose in my skin. My ass was hot now, and each smack of Liam's hands left a bloom of fresh pain. To my surprise, each burst of pain was soon followed by a jolt of pure pleasure. It made my core feel heavy and achy, desperate to be filled.

All the noise in my head began to recede, leaving all my focus on this room, this man, and the sensation of him spanking me.

I realized that Liam's words from earlier were correct: a little pain added to the excitement.

At some point, I began lifting my ass to meet his hand and grinding my clit against his leg with each downward stroke, trying to get myself off on his thigh. I was close to coming just from that, and of course the bastard sensed it and stopped.

He rubbed his palm gently over my skin, soothing me while I silently fumed about being denied yet another orgasm. Yet when his fingers slid between my thighs again, I willingly opened for him, welcoming me inside.

"Your ass looks incredible all red from my palm," he told me as he moved his finger up and down my channel.

In the silence of the room, I could hear how wet I was. My face flamed with embarrassment.

"You're dripping for me, Coco."

His voice was filled with a masculine satisfaction that would have grated on me if I wasn't so overcome with lust.

Liam inserted one finger into my opening, pumping in and out roughly. I sighed, pushing back against his hand, and then he added a second finger, bringing me closer and closer to release. My breathing quickened as I fucked myself against his fingers.

"Do you want to come?" he asked.

"Yes," I gasped.

I wanted to come right now more than I'd ever wanted to come in my life, this I was absolutely sure of.

"Ask me nicely."

I stiffened as I remembered his earlier words about making me beg. When I didn't respond, he pressed his thumb against my swollen clit and gently curved his fingers inside me, stroking the rough patch of skin on my internal wall that I knew – he knew – would drive me right over the edge.

I moaned, the sound high and needy in the silent room.

Then he paused again.

"Ask me nicely," he said again.

By this point I was shaking, so desperate to come that I was willing to do anything – anything – to get relief. So when his fingers stroked my G-spot again I couldn't help but yell out, "Please Liam, please let me come!"

I had no shame anymore. I just needed relief.

And when Liam whispered, "Come for me Coco, come all over my hand like a good girl," I did just that.

Chapter Nine

"I should probably head home."

Liam squeezed his arm around me tighter. "You've only had one orgasm," he reminded me.

"And a nap."

I'd come so hard after he spanked me and finger-fucked me that I'd damn near passed out. I hadn't even been aware of Liam drawing me up on the bed and covering me with a blanket until I'd woken up half an hour later.

His hand snaked down beneath the blanket, cupping my mound. I was instantly wet again. Or still. I didn't know anymore.

I rolled onto my back and opened my legs, then yelped as my ass hit the sheets. It was a little sorer than I'd expected.

Liam chuckled, making me want to punch him in the junk. Speaking of junk...

"Do you want me to, um, take care of you?"

He titled his head. "Take care of me?"

"Suck you off or something. It's only fair."

"Everything doesn't have to be tit for tat you know."

I didn't know. My ex had always been very adamant that if he got me off with his fingers or mouth it was in exchange for a blow job. Unless it was my birthday of course.

Liam shifted so he was laying on top of me, his legs sliding between mine, his hard cock pressed against my pussy.

"You're still dressed."

"I'm going to stay that way."

I frowned.

"I'm not going to fuck you tonight, Coco. That would make it too easy for you to write this off as just sex. And this is not just sex."

He rolled his hips, sliding the fabric against my pussy lips. My breath hitched. Without conscious thought, I bent my knees and spread them wide.

"You want more?" he asked as he basically dry humped me.

"Yeah."

"Do you trust me?"

"Not really," I joked.

Except it wasn't really a joke. In fairness, I trusted him more than I did most people.

He studied my face. "You don't trust anyone, do you?"

I shook my head. "I learned a long time ago that I can only rely on myself."

I felt the most ridiculous urge to cry, which was weird, because I never cried.

Liam shifted so he could brush my hair off my face. It was a mess after what we'd done earlier.

"I guess I'll just have to earn your trust," he whispered.

Liam lowered his head, giving me a kiss that was soft and sweet, completely different than the way he'd kissed me before. Slowly, gently, he deepened the kiss until his tongue slid against mine.

I reached up and tangled my fingers into his short brown hair, holding him closer.

We kissed like that for a long time, like we were two teenagers making out on the couch, and when he finally pulled away, I felt almost sad.

He shifted downward, pushing the blanket out of the way to expose my bare breasts. He cupped them and pushed them together before his gaze returned to my face.

"Someday I'm going to fuck your breasts, Coco. And with every thrust you'll take my cock into your mouth, just a little bit, until you're desperate for me to fuck your throat. But I won't, not then, instead

I'll spread my cum all over your face and your beautiful tits until I've marked you as mine."

I couldn't help the moan that ripped from my throat.

"I had no idea you were so filthy."

"I had no idea you'd like dirty talk so much," he rejoined, lowering his head to take one nipple between his lips.

I expected him to suckle me, but instead he held the nipple between his teeth while he ran the top of his tongue back and forth against the edge of the nipple. It was a small move, but effective at ratcheting up my excitement quickly.

By the time he moved to the other nipple, I was shoving my breasts upward like an offering.

He kissed down my abdomen, and I resisted the urge to suck it in. I wasn't as lean as I was the first time he saw me naked all those years ago. He didn't seem to mind though.

I giggled as he licked inside my belly button.

"That tickles," I protested.

He ignored me, licking me some more before finally, finally, shoving his shoulders between my legs. The instant his tongue slid between my lower lips, my hips punched up into the air and I gasped.

Somehow I was already sensitive, my entire core feeling engorged and swollen, ready to go.

Liam looked up at me from between my legs, and I could see my moisture glistening on his lips.

"Don't come until I give you permission."

"Is it going to be like this every time?" I whined. "Because I don't like this game."

"I think you do."

I did. I totally did. The way he'd been edging me and teasing me for days had me feeling more sexually aware and hornier than I'd been even as a teenager. I guessed I didn't mind giving him control of my orgasms if they were going to be like the one I'd had earlier. Or the one yesterday.

Not that I would share that with Liam. I didn't need him thinking he had the upper hand with me, even if he did.

Every other thought went out of my head as Liam began eating me out. He spread my lips wide so he could dive in deep, his tongue exploring every nook and cranny before he concentrated his attention on my clit. He circled it several times, then began tapping it with his tongue in short bursts.

"Liam!" I gripped his hair, trying to focus him where I needed him the most.

He kept licking and tapping, taking me higher and higher until...

"You can't come."

I sagged to the bed as he lifted his head.

"What the fuck?"

"You're going to need to work for this one."

"I thought you didn't want me to suck you off?"

"That's not what I mean."

He pushed up to sit on his heels.

"Play with your tits."

"What?"

"I want to watch you."

We stared at each other until I finally looked away with a huff. I lowered my hands to cup my breasts, squeezing them a few times before stroking around the areolas, gradually moving closer to the nipples, just like I liked.

I heard the sound of a zipper and when I looked up, Liam was releasing his cock from his boxers. It looked red and angry and painfully erect. I licked my lips.

"Next time," he promised, giving himself a hard stroke.

He nodded towards my chest. "Keep going."

I began pulling and pinching my breasts while Liam watched, slowly stroking his cock. As my excitement increased, my hips started rolling of their own volition.

"Touch your pussy. Get yourself ready, but don't come."

I was too far gone now to do anything but obey him. I slid my hands downward, resting one on my mound while the other slid inside my channel, moving back and forth. I was slicker than I'd ever been in my life, and my fingers moved easily.

"Put your finger inside yourself," Liam ordered, his voice rough. "Just one."

I slid my middle finger inside my channel and started pumping in and out while I teased my clit with my other hand. I was so close, my pussy was clenching tight against my finger, desperate to be filled.

"I need..."

"What do you need, baby?" Liam's hand was getting a little faster as he stroked his cock.

"More."

"Put in another finger."

I added my index finger, pumping as deep as I could reach.

"Curl your fingers, see if you can find your special slot."

I moaned loudly, my hips flying upwards, and Liam chuckled. "I guess you found it."

I kept stroking deep inside myself while stroking my clit, shaking with the effort to keep from coming.

"Liam. Please. I need to come."

I was beyond pride at this point.

"Soon, baby. Give your little clit a nice pinch for me."

I complied immediately, feeling the first trembles of my orgasm rolling through my core.

"Please Liam, please."

He groaned as his own orgasm approached.

"Good girl. You can come."

When I just whined, mindlessly fucking my fingers, he added. "Come now!"

His words ended with a groan as cum jetted over his fingers, dripping down onto the bed. He groaned my name, staring at my fingers thrusting in and out of my pussy as he found his release.

Meanwhile, I watched him thrust against his hand, spurting more of his seed, and I let go, wailing with the force of my orgasm. My back arched off the bed, and I shook with the strength of the pleasure that overwhelmed me.

When I was done, I sagged back on the bed, closing my eyes tightly. I'd never masturbated with anyone before, and I was shocked at how hot it was. I heard Liam shuffling around, returning with a warm cloth that he used to clean me up, then he got back onto the bed and pulled me close.

As I snuggled into his chest, I wished I could stay there forever.

Chapter Ten

"You're home late."

I jumped as I heard my mother's voice call out to me from the living room. After being on my own since I was eighteen, I wasn't used to having someone tracking my comings and goings. While I appreciated that my parents had offered to let me move back in with them after I'd lost everything, I really could not get into my own place fast enough.

My mother studied my face, a small smile quirking up the corners of her lips.

"Looks like you had fun."

Before I could stop myself, I smoothed my hand down my hair. Oh. My. God! Could my mother tell I'd been having sex? Please don't let her ask...please don't let her ask...

"So, you and Liam, huh?"

My knees buckled and I dropped into a chair.

"What? No. I mean, what are you talking about?"

Mom looked amused.

"Your father saw you leaving the office with him, and here you are, coming home at one in the morning, looking well...loved."

My heart was racing in panic. What the fuck was I supposed to say right now? This is exactly why I hadn't wanted to go out with Liam. It was impossible to keep secrets in Posen, where everyone knew everyone's business.

When I didn't answer, Mom leaned back on the couch, still studying me.

"You know, your father and I never wanted anything more than for you and Paula to find the kind of love that we have with each other. When Paula got together with Liam, we were surprised."

"Surprised?"

"We'd always assumed that you two would end up together. You seemed to have a connection that wasn't there for him and Paula. Right up until their wedding day we thought maybe Liam would realize that he was marrying the wrong sister."

I gasped.

"But then they went through with the wedding, and you married Daniel, and we thought maybe we were wrong. But I see now we weren't. Liam and Paula were a disaster, and as for Daniel, I know I shouldn't speak ill of the dead, but he was an asshole. I never liked him."

"What? How did you know? I never told any of you about the things that Daniel did."

"We have eyes, dear. And friends in the city. We heard the rumors."

My face burned with humiliation.

"That's all on him, Colleen, not you. The question is, now that you and Liam have found your way back to each other, what are you going to do? Not everyone gets a second chance."

I stood up and started pacing.

"What am I going to do? What can I do?" I asked. "He's Dad's business partner and my sister's ex-husband. It's messy as fuck."

"Love is messy. Things weren't always easy but if you love him, the messy part will be worth it."

I shook my head.

"No, I can't do this to Paula."

"She and Liam have been divorced for a long time," she reminded me. "They're good friends now, and I'm betting she'll want him to be happy as much as she'll want her sister to be happy. Finally."

My mother's words echoed in my head the next day. Liam was in court, so I didn't see him at the office, although we'd texted briefly this morning. He'd sent me a sweet good morning text that I couldn't help but smile about.

Later that day I was back in my childhood bedroom reading before dinner when I heard a knock.

"Come on in, Mom."

Just like that day two weeks ago, the door opened to reveal Liam. He was still wearing his suit, his tie loosened, which immediately brought me back to the night in my office when he'd tied my wrists.

"What are you doing here?"

I saw a flash of hurt in his eyes at my wary tone.

"Your mother invited me for dinner."

I nodded. "She's playing matchmaker."

He smirked. "I wondered. Especially when she sent me up here to tell you that dinner would be ready in half an hour, so we had plenty of time to," he made quotation marks with his fingers, "talk."

"My parents know we were together last night," I told him. "Mom was waiting up for me when I got home."

He stepped closer, cupping my cheek with one hand.

"What's going on in that head of yours, beautiful?"

"I need to get my own place, for one thing."

"You should move in with me." He said it casually, like it was no big deal.

"I'm not moving in with you!"

"Why not? It's going to happen eventually."

Somehow, he'd managed to back me against the wall when I wasn't paying attention. I didn't realize it until my butt connected with the drywall behind me. Liam lowered his head until our lips were less than an inch apart.

"I have plans for us Coco."

"What kind of plans?" I whispered.

"We're going to move in together, and when you're ready, I'm going to marry you."

I shook my head, the motion making our noses rub against each other.

"I'm never going to get married again. And there's no way I'm going to stand at the altar where people watched you marry my sister and have people whispering about us."

"We can elope."

"It's all so easy for you, isn't it? You'll be the stud who bagged two sisters and I'll be the pathetic slut who took her sister's sloppy seconds."

His brown eyes darkened.

"You'll never be sloppy seconds."

He kissed me then, and damned if the very touch of his lips against mine didn't make me melt against him. My arms moved around his shoulders as if they had a mind of their own, and I rolled my hips to press against his growing erection. Our tongues tangled, and Liam tunneled his fingers into my long brown hair, tilting my head to get better access to my mouth.

I could kiss this man for hours, but I wanted more.

Pulling back, I met his eyes.

"Fuck me, Liam. I need you."

The second his hands moved to his zipper I shoved down my jeans and yoga pants and kicked them away.

"Are you sure?" he asked.

I nodded. "Just be quiet. I don't want my parents to hear."

He smirked. "You're the one who's a screamer, baby."

I smacked his shoulder. "I've never screamed during sex in my life."

"You've come close," he argued. "Just last night in fact."

"Do you want to be right, or do you want to fuck me?"

"Fuck you. I definitely choose fuck you."

He dropped his pants to his ankles, then shoved his boxers down too, revealing his thick cock. I reached for it, wrapping my fingers around his length and giving it a firm stroke from root to tip. Liam groaned, pushing into my hand, and I did it again.

I loved knowing that I had this effect on him, that I wasn't alone in this crazy passion.

He reached for my thighs, boosting me up against the wall, and I locked my ankles behind his waist.

"Hold on, baby. This isn't going to be gentle."

"I don't want gentle," I told him. "I want it fast and hard."

He slammed his cock inside me in one long thrust and we both groaned. "Your wish is my command."

Despite his words, he paused for a moment, giving me time to adjust.

"I thought our first time would be a little more romantic," he said ruefully. "Maybe on a bed."

"I don't need romantic, I need real. Besides, that little twin bed scarcely holds me, and there's no way I'm explaining to my mother how it got broken."

He groaned. "Please don't talk about your mother when my cock is inside you."

"Why?" I teased. "Do you want to talk about your mother instead?"

He crushed his lips down on mine in an obvious attempt to shut me up. Obvious but effective. His tongue thrust into my mouth in rhythm with the way his cock was thrusting into my channel. I gripped his shoulders for leverage, pressed my back firmly against the wall, and rolled my hips forward to meet him with every stroke.

Liam pounded into me roughly, filling me up with his cock in a way I'd been craving since the last time he fucked me all those years ago. We were at the perfect angle for him to slide against my clit with every stroke and in an impossibly short time I could feel the first glimmers of my orgasm coming down my spine.

Liam could feel it too because he broke away long enough to say, "Come for me, Coco. I'm not going to last much longer."

Then he lowered his head and bit into my shoulder and my breath stuttered in my lungs as wave after wave of pleasure rolled through my body.

"Liam!" I gasped. "You feel so good."

His pace quickened as he sought his own release. He was pounding into me hard enough now that my head was bouncing against the wall.

He slid one hand behind my head and then let out a long, low groan as he came.

Liam pushed inside me deeply, releasing his cum in long bursts, painting my womb with his warmth. I quivered around him, riding out the end of my own orgasm and shaking with the force of it.

When he was done Liam stood perfectly still, his head buried in my shoulder, his body still pinning me against the wall.

He pulled back slowly.

"Come home with me tonight."

"But my parents..."

His voice lowered and he gave me a stern look that made yet another rush of moisture flood my pussy. One corner of his mouth quirked, telling me that he was fully aware of his effect on me.

"Come home with me tonight," he ordered.

"Okay. But we need to talk to Paula. Soon."

Chapter Eleven

"When is Paula back in town?" I asked my mother. "I texted her a couple of times, but she didn't respond."

My sister had gone on some work trip that involved a Caribbean island. It all sounded a bit shady to me, but Paula had assured me that a lot of the more successful start-up companies would offer these kinds of trips as perks.

Mom gave me a sympathetic look. She knew that I was nervous about telling Paula about my relationship with Liam, and she also knew that I'd spent each of the last five nights at his house. I needed to get to my sister before the small-town gossips did.

"Tomorrow," Mom responded. "I was just looking at the travel confirmation she sent me before her trip."

"It will all be fine, Colleen, I promise you. Paula got over Liam a long time ago, and I'm pretty sure she's secretly dating someone at the office."

I looked at her in surprise. "How on Earth would you know that?"

Paula worked several towns away and was in the tech industry.

"I have spies everywhere, dear."

Later that night, over dinner I told Liam about the conversation. We'd fallen into a domestic routine, having dinner together each night before fucking each other's brains out. The sex was hot and sometimes kinky and always satisfying.

"I texted Paula and invited her to have dinner the night she gets back. Hopefully she won't be too tired. I figured we could tell her then."

Liam nodded. "It's going to be fine, Coco. Trust me."

"That's what Mom said too, but she doesn't know what happened before either."

"Paula doesn't need to know either."

"I think she does," I said stubbornly. "If she ever finds out and we didn't tell her, it's going to be bad."

"It was twelve years ago, and she hasn't found out yet," he reminded me. "We're the only two who know the truth, and I say we take it to our grave."

"No."

"Coco, be reasonable. If we tell her, it's going to hurt her a lot and there's no reason for it. We'd only be telling her to get absolution or something. It feels selfish to hurt her like that after all this time."

"I don't know, Liam. I just don't feel right about it."

He reached for my hand and pulled me off the couch.

"Let's sleep on it. Right now, I've got a present for you."

I followed him into his bedroom, ignoring the giant king-sized bed where I'd slept snuggled against him the last five nights.

"What kind of present?"

The mischievous look on his face told me that the present was not going to be a bouquet of flowers. He reached into a drawer and pulled out a smallish box, placing it in my palm. I looked through the clear plastic packaging and gasped.

"A butt plug? No way."

It was small and looked to be made out of pink silicone, shaped like a little Christmas tree, but it still looked intimidating.

"I think you're going to like it."

"I am not going to like it. I told you before, no anal."

"But then I stuck my finger in your ass, and you came your brains out."

"Only because you had me tied to the bed."

He raised one eyebrow. "Do you need me to spank the truth out of you?"

My ass was still a little tender from last night, so I decided to answer honestly.

"Fine, maybe I liked the finger thing, but this is different."

He walked closer, resting his palms on my shoulder. "Coco, have we done one thing that you haven't liked?"

I shook my head. "I guess not."

"We don't have to do anything you don't want to, but so far, you've been enjoying trying new things and I've been enjoying it too. There's nothing more beautiful than the look on your face when you submit to me, when you stop thinking and just let yourself feel the pleasure that I'm giving you."

He slid his hands down and cupped my ass, smirking when I winced.

"You thought you wouldn't like being spanked either and you were practically begging for it last night."

It had been a bad day yesterday. I'd signed the final papers on my house, turning it over to the bank, and I'd lost one of my freelance clients. By the time I'd gotten here, I was so riled up that when Liam asked if I wanted a spanking to calm down I'd practically whipped off my pants. Then I begged him for more when he tried to stop.

I had no idea spanking could be so therapeutic. The ability to get out of my own head and just *feel* was a gift I never knew that I needed.

"Fine I'll try the plug, but if I don't like it, you need to remove it right away and never ever bring it up again."

He nodded. "Deal."

Liam kissed me then, slow and deep, his mouth dominating mine until we broke apart breathless. My nipples were hardened points against my shirt, and just like every time this man touched me, my panties were already soaked.

I pulled his tee shirt over his head, tossing it behind us, and went to work on his belt. After I unbuckled it, Liam pulled it out of the loops and threw it down, his pants and boxers soon following. I licked my lips, remembering the other night when he'd used that belt to tie my hands behind my back and then ordered me to drop to my knees and suck his cock.

From the expression on Liam's face, he was remembering it too.

He motioned for me to turn around, and then me a quick smack on the ass. Fortunately, I was still wearing pants, but not for long.

Liam pulled down my jeans and panties, tapping my ankles so I'd step out. Once we were both naked, he gave me a little push.

"Lay on your belly on the bed. Keep your feet on the floor."

It was still hard to reconcile that the easy-going guy I loved to hang out with had this other side, a side where he liked to take control, to spank me or tie me down, and make me beg for an orgasm. It was also hard to reconcile that even though I was incredibly independent, I liked this game we were playing.

It would never be okay in real life, but in the safety of the bedroom, I was all for it.

I lowered my torso onto the bed, turning my face to one side. I heard a drawer open and then Liam tossed a tube of lube on the bed near me. I thought he'd go right for the plug, but instead he leaned over me, surrounding me, and nipped my ear.

Slowly, torturously, he made his way down my neck to my shoulder, nipping me with his teeth, then licking the area to soothe the stinging. My mind flashed back to the night in my office when he said he wanted to bite every inch of my body. I guess tonight was the night.

He bit and licked his way down my back, zigzagging from side to side, as if trying to make sure no part of me was neglected. When he got to my ass the bites got sharper.

"Ow!" I cried as he took a nice bite out of my left cheek.

He licked around the bite, mumbling against my skin, "Shush. I want to mark you as mine."

Damned if that didn't bring me close to an orgasm all by itself.

He left several more stinging bites on my ass, the pain from the pinch of his teeth sooth turning to red hot arousal. By the time he was biting his way across the bottom of my butt cheeks I was pushing up to meet him, begging for more.

I whimpered when he stopped, but then he slid his fingers into my slit, spreading my moisture before inserting a finger. He thrust in and out a few times, then added a second finger. When I was so close to coming that I could almost taste it, he stopped. I groaned in frustration.

Delayed orgasm was practically a calling card with this guy.

I heard the sound of the lube cap right before I felt a glob of it land on my ass crack. Liam slid a finger between my cheeks, spreading the lube.

"Hold yourself open for me baby," he instructed. "I'll get you ready."

Already half gone with my impending orgasm, I didn't hesitate to comply. I reached back and spread my cheeks while Liam added more lube, circling my asshole with it. When he pushed one finger inside me, I gasped.

"Relax," he said, giving me a pinch with his other hand.

His finger slid in farther and he started pumping in and out, prepping me. It felt weird, but not unpleasant.

By the time he pulled out, I was panting again just from that stimulation.

"The key is when I insert the plug, you need to relax your muscles and bear down a bit."

"Bear down?"

"Like you're going to poop."

"Eww!" I squealed. "That is not sexy."

"Oh I'll make it sexy for you, baby, don't worry."

Somewhere along the way he'd started calling me 'baby' in the bedroom, and honestly, I didn't hate it.

Liam lubed up the plug, resting it between my cheeks, then went back to fucking my pussy with his finger. He moved slowly at first, then quickened his pace, adding a second finger and then a third until my pussy was stuffed with his questing fingers.

He shifted, and I felt the tip of the plug press against my pucker. Automatically I stiffened. Liam immediately removed his fingers from my pussy and gave me a sharp smack on the side of my hip.

"Relax!" he ordered.

The tip of the plug broached my opening.

"Good girl," he praised me.

Another thing I'd discovered this week: I apparently had a praise kink because nothing made me hotter than Liam calling me a 'good girl' in that deliciously deep voice of his.

I'd learned more about myself and what I liked sexually in less than one week with Liam than I had in all the years I'd been with my husband.

He kneaded my ass cheek, giving me time to adjust, and when my inner muscles relaxed, he ordered, "Bear down."

I did, and the plug was in.

"How does it feel?" he asked.

"Weird."

Then he began sliding it in and out, fucking me with it, while his fingers returned to my pussy.

"Holy. Shit."

I felt completely full, the dual action of his fingers in my pussy and the plug in my ass electrifying everything below the waist.

"Liam," I cried. "I need..."

"Let go, Coco," he told me. "Let go."

My orgasm crashed through me, and I thrashed against his fingers. Liam banded an arm around the top of my ass to hold me in place and he continued his dual assault on my body. I thrashed and cried and possibly saw God himself as I rode the waves of my orgasm.

When it was all over, I collapsed against the bed, gulping for air, tears streaming down my face from the intensity of it all. Leaving the butt plug inside me, Liam crawled up to my side and gave me a sweet kiss on the lips.

"So the butt plug is a hit, huh?"

Chapter Twelve

I was waiting on my sister's porch when she returned from the airport. She got out of the Uber, dragging her suitcase behind her, and gave me a quizzical look.

"What's up, Colleen?"

"I know you just got back, but I really need to talk to you."

"Okay, but I really need to take a quick shower first. That flight was hell."

I waited in the kitchen, sipping at a bottle of water I'd swiped from her fridge. Liam had thought we should tell Paula together, but I'd insisted on coming alone. We needed to handle this sister-to-sister.

"What's wrong, little sister?" Paula asked, coming back wearing sleep shorts and a tank top, her long hair hanging wet around her shoulders. "You look pensive."

"I have something to tell you," I started. "You're not going to like this."

"Is this about Liam?" she asked, looking amused.

My gaze shot up to hers. "What?"

"This is a small town Colleen, people have noticed you together."

Crap. I'd refused to do too much with Liam out of the house for this very reason.

"Besides, Mom told me when you came back that she wanted to try to fix you two up. I told her to give you some time to recover from everything that had happened, but when I heard you two were hanging out, I figured you and Liam had gotten together on your own."

"I'm so sorry Paula, I wanted you to hear about it from me."

She waved her hand dismissively. "I think it's great."

I choked on my own spit.

"You do?"

She nodded.

"You're okay with me dating your ex-husband?" I clarified.

"I mean, it would probably be weird if we'd just broken up, but we divorced years ago. Liam and I are good friends now and we had the most amicable divorce in the history of divorces. He's a good guy, Colleen, why wouldn't I want you to be with someone good for once, especially after everything that jackass Daniel put you through?"

I hadn't expected my sister to be so cool about this, but I suspected that was going to change.

"There's more."

Paula looked at my face and stood up. "Sounds like we might need some tequila."

She brought a bottle to the table and poured us each a shot. I downed mine in one gulp, relishing the hot sting of the alcohol in my throat.

"When you first started dating Liam back in school, I was jealous. Even though the three of us still hung out together, it felt like I was losing my best friend and my sister in one fell swoop, especially when you two left for college."

Paula nodded but didn't respond.

"I convinced myself that I was in love with Liam, and that he loved me."

I didn't mention that I'd thought that because he'd told me he loved me. No sense digging the knife in.

"Before your wedding, I went to Liam and I begged him not to marry you. I tried to convince him that he should be with me instead."

"I hope he let you down easy."

Paula must have seen something in my eyes because she said, "He let you down easy right? He told you that he loved me and was going to marry me?"

I couldn't lie to her. "He was...conflicted."

"I knew it!" Paula practically yelled the words. "I knew he had a thing for you! I asked him about it more than once and he denied it, but my intuition was right all along."

"He loved you," I said in a small voice. "In his own way. He told me so."

"Well in retrospect, I wish he would have listened to you, Colleen. It would have been better if we'd never gotten married. Our divorce may have been amicable, but it was still painful. And the marriage wasn't a good one."

"I'm sorry that I betrayed you like that Paula. I don't have an excuse other than I was young and foolish."

"Don't worry about it, it's not like you slept with him or something."

Everything in me froze. My sister and I locked eyes, and I knew the moment she saw the truth there.

"You slept with my husband?!?"

She pushed out of her chair so quickly that it fell to the ground with a loud crash. Her face was flushed red with anger and hurt.

"No! No, I did NOT sleep with him when you were married. I didn't see him again or even talk to him after the wedding – not even once—until a couple of weeks ago when I moved back to town."

"Wait, so this is why you two were so adamant about avoiding each other all these years, because you'd had an affair?"

"Not an affair. It was one time. Well, one night. That's all, I swear it. I'm so sorry I betrayed you, Paula. It was a horrible, selfish thing to do, and I would do anything to take it back."

Her hands wrapped around the back of another chair, knuckles white, and I had the sense she was wishing that was my neck right now.

"Tell me everything from the beginning," she instructed, her words slow and carefully enunciated. "I deserve to hear it all."

I brushed away the tears that were falling down my face, reminding myself that I wasn't the one who deserved to cry.

"Liam and I had always been close, as you know. Two days before the wedding we'd spent the day running around doing wedding stuff while you and your friends were at the spa."

"I remember."

"I went back to his place to help bag up the rest of those Jordan almonds for the reception, and he confessed he was having cold feet. That he loved you but wasn't sure he was *in* love with you."

I paused, and Paula made an impatient gesture with her hand.

"He kissed me, and one thing led to another, and we ended up spending the night together. When we got up in the morning, Liam was freaking out about what to do. I went home and then later, well later I tried to get him to choose me. But he said he'd made a commitment to you, and he was going through with it, which of course was the right thing to do, so I did my best to get through the wedding and I left town while you were on your honeymoon just to make sure that nothing would happen again."

I gulped in a breath.

"Is that all?"

"Yes. I never saw him again. Never talked to him. Never asked anyone about him. I just got on with my life, married Daniel, and moved on."

"And now you're moving on again—with my ex."

I flinched.

"I'll break it off with him Paula. You're way more important to me than he is."

"Not important enough to keep you from fucking him when we were together though," she said bitterly.

"I am so sorry. I never meant to hurt you. I'm so ashamed of how I behaved, even all these years later I hate myself for what I did."

I stifled a sob.

"I know what it's like, I know how it feels to have someone you thought loved you cheat on you. When I found out about Daniel and his pregnant girlfriend, my very first thought was that what this girl did, it's exactly what I did to you."

The room fell silent for what felt like hours but was probably just a couple of minutes. I watched my sister stare at the floor, her eyes wide and shell-shocked. When she finally looked up, I knew what she was going to say before the words left her lips.

"Get out."

Chapter Thirteen

"Are you skipping work again?"

My mom didn't bother knocking before she stuck her head in the bedroom. I pulled the blanket up over my head so I wouldn't have to look at her.

"Yes."

"How about some pancakes then?"

"I'm not hungry, Mom." I gentled my tone. "Thanks though. I just need to be alone."

Ignoring that subtle hint, Mom came in and sat at the edge of my bed. When I ignored her, she pulled the blanket down.

"Liam stopped by again this morning. I told him you were still indisposed."

"I told him I didn't want to talk to him," I reminded her, the same way I'd done yesterday and the day before. "We broke up."

"I don't think he's broken up, dear. Your father said he's been a bear at the office. He's really hurting."

"You know who's really hurting? Paula!" I snapped.

"Yes, I've spoken to her as well. It was a shock for her to hear what happened after all these years, but I know my daughter. She'll get over it."

"She told you what happened?" I squeaked, pulling the blanket back up over my head.

"Well honestly I'd mostly pieced it together between what you'd told me and something Liam said to your father, but yes, Paula told me that you and Liam slept together before the wedding."

"I'm the worst person ever," I moaned.

"Colleen Elizabeth Leahy," Mom chided. "You can't just wallow in bed like this. It's been three days now. I understand you did something terrible and there's absolutely no excuse for what you and Liam did, but

69

it was also more than twelve years ago. You're not the same person you were back then. Neither is Liam, and neither is your sister."

"She's never going to forgive me, Mom, and I don't blame her."

"Let me ask you this, if you found out that Paula slept with Daniel before your wedding, knowing how your marriage would end up, would you be able to forgive your sister?"

"I'd be able to forgive her not because of Daniel but because she's my sister. I would judge her on the totality of her actions."

"And Paula will get there eventually, but in the meantime, I can't have you wallowing in this bedroom like a petulant teenager. You're a grown woman with a job. Now get your ass up and come downstairs so I can make you some chocolate chip pancakes!"

I sat up and for the first time since I arrived at Paula's house the other day, I smiled.

Mom wrinkled her nose. "Ugh, take a shower first. We can't eat breakfast with you smelling like that."

After a shower I was feeling at least half human. I was surprised when I got downstairs to see my father sitting at the table, reading something on his tablet.

"Dad? Aren't you going to work?"

"It's Saturday."

I looked between him and my mother. "Then why did you ask me if I was going to work, Mom?"

She shrugged. "Seemed like a good way to get you out of bed."

I poured myself a cup of coffee and sat at the table, staring into the liquid pensively.

"I heard you broke up with Liam," my father said quietly.

"No offense Dad, but I don't want to talk about it."

"Maybe you should just listen then," he said sternly.

My head snapped up. Dad was rarely stern.

"It's a rare gift, finding true love. Even rarer to find it, lose it, and then find it again. You need to figure out how to fix this situation, Colleen, because love probably won't find you a third time."

When I didn't answer he added, "Did you know Liam is reconsidering buying me out of the practice now? He says it's too painful to be here living in Posen if you don't want to be with him."

"I want to be with him, okay?" I snapped. "But not if it hurts Paula."

"Then make things right with your sister so you can be with the man you love."

After breakfast I texted my sister asking her to let me know when we could talk more. To my surprise, she suggested that I come over that evening – and bring Liam.

"We broke up," I texted her.

"Well un-break up and get his ass there. And bring pizza," was her response.

Sighing deeply, I texted Liam that Paula wanted to see us. I wasn't surprised when my phone rang with an incoming call.

"Hi Liam."

"How are you, Coco?" His voice was thick with concern. "I've been worried about you."

"Paula wants us to come over tonight at five and talk about...everything. She says to bring pizza."

He let out a whoosh of air.

"Oh good, that means she's going to forgive us."

"What?"

"Remember I told you about that time we split up? She invited me over a few weeks later and told me to bring pizza. We hashed everything out over pepperoni pizza, and then agreed to go to counseling. It's a sign that she's ready to forgive us."

I tried not to focus on the glimmer of hope that brought out in me.

"Okay, do you want to pick up the pizza or shall I?"

"I'll pick up the pizza and then swing by and pick you up too."

"No."

"You live between Paula's house and the pizza place anyway."

"No. I'll walk."

"Coco." The stern tone in his voice made my pussy tingle.

"Liam," I sassed back. "We're not together anymore. You don't get to use that tone with me."

"We'll see about that," he said stubbornly.

"I'll meet you at Paula's," I said firmly, hanging up before he could say anything else.

I was so nervous about the meeting with my sister I did something I never did: go for a run. I dug out my long-neglected running shoes, changed into a pair of shorts and a sports tank, and ran until I was weak-legged with exhaustion. Then I took another shower and got ready to head over to my sister's house.

I'd walked about four blocks when Liam pulled up next to me.

"Get in."

"I'm walking thank you."

I kept walking, and he drove slowly next to me.

"Get in."

When I ignored him, he yelled out the window, "Do you want me to spank your ass red again, is that it?"

"Liam!" I pulled open the passenger door with a stern glare. "What the actual fuck? You want everyone in town to hear you talking like that?"

He shrugged. "It worked."

I crossed my arms and slid down in my seat, staring out the window and ignoring him on the short drive over to my sister's house. In the enclosed space of the car, I could smell the pizza that was sitting on the back seat and a scent that was uniquely Liam. I'd missed that scent.

We stood side-by-side on the front porch, Liam holding a pizza box in one hand, his other hand just barely touching my waist, like he wanted to offer support but was afraid I'd push him away if he touched me.

When Paula opened the door, she looked subdued, but her eyes were clear.

"Come on in."

We followed her into the kitchen, setting out plates, and opening bottles of beer in silence. Once we were all seated, I couldn't take it anymore.

"Thanks for being willing to talk to us, Paula," I said politely like I was an insurance salesman instead of a woman who'd slept with her sister's fiancé.

"I've thought a lot about what happened," Paula started, pausing to take a bite of pizza. My sister was not one to let anything get in the way of her and cheesy carbs.

"I know you are both remorseful and I also believe that neither of you would do something like that again."

"No!" I said.

"We wouldn't," Liam said at the same time. "It was a terrible mistake and I've regretted it every single day, but we're different people now. Nothing like that would happen again."

Paula nodded, taking another bite of pizza.

"Mom told me you two broke up."

"We did," I said.

"We're just on a break," Liam contradicted, sending me a stubborn look.

"In that case, I have the solution for how we can all move past this."

"What is it?" I asked hopefully.

"I'm going to fuck Liam."

Chapter Fourteen

"I'm going to fuck Liam."

"What?" Liam and I spoke in unison.

My sister burst out laughing.

"Oh my God! You should see your faces!"

She pointed between us.

"I'm just kidding, obviously. Besides, I'm kind of seeing someone."

I remembered Mom saying she thought Paula was dating someone at her work, but I didn't want to rock the boat by asking right now.

"Look, I'm not going to lie, hearing what you did really hurt me, and I'm pissed about it. But it was also a long time ago and we were all so young back then, it doesn't feel right to hold you accountable for anything that happened when you were twenty-two. You were just a baby, really."

"I knew what I was doing though Paula, I appreciate you giving us an out, but I was old enough to know better."

She pointed at Liam. "Tell me you never slept with or kissed anyone else while we were married or dating."

He held up his hand in what I was guessing was a scout gesture. "Never, I swear it."

Paula's eyes swung in my direction. "Did you kiss or sleep with any of my other boyfriends?"

"God no."

She raised her eyebrows.

"No offense."

In my defense, every guy she'd dated besides Liam was a total loser. I only hoped the new guy was a decent one.

"In that case, I forgive you and we should never talk about this again."

She resumed eating pizza like she was coming off of a no carb diet.

"That's it?" I asked. "We're all good?"

"We're all good," Paula confirmed.

I couldn't help but look at her suspiciously.

"Come on now, eat your pizza before I change my mind."

She pointed a slice of pizza at Liam.

"And you can un-break up with this guy now. I know y'all are in love. Quit being weird about it."

"See?" Liam sent me a smile.

"Shut up." I told him, but when he took my hand, I didn't pull away.

"Do you think you can convince her to move in with me too?" Liam asked.

I elbowed him in the ribs.

"Only if I get to be your Best Woman at the wedding."

"We are not having a wedding," I protested.

"Sure we are."

I sighed deeply and my sister burst out laughing. "Yeah, I'm going to enjoy this."

We finished up the pizza, talking and laughing about nothing important, the easy camaraderie between us reminiscent of when we were all younger and just friends.

Paula practically pushed us out the door afterward, telling us that her new guy was coming over after he got out of a family party. She looked excited about him, and I hoped that she found the easy love that she'd been looking for – that we'd both been looking for – just like my parents had.

Without thinking, I followed Liam to his car. I knew we needed to talk so I wasn't surprised when he turned up the street towards his house instead of taking me back to my parents' house. I was drained by everything that happened with my sister though and wasn't sure I was up for any more heavy discussion.

Liam, as always, seemed to tune into just what I needed.

"Want to watch a few episodes of The Office?"

I sent him a grateful smile. "Yeah."

We cuddled together on the couch until eventually I was ready to talk.

"I'm not ready to move in," I told him at the end of one episode. "But I think I will be. Someday soon."

He squeezed my shoulders. "Someday soon works for me."

"I have an idea," he said. "I'm going to lean you over the back of the couch and fuck you from behind while we watch another episode. You'll keep your eyes on the TV at all times and if you can get through the whole thing without coming, I'll give you a special treat."

"Is the special treat your cock?" I asked saucily. "Because I've already had it and it's an average treat at best."

In an instant I was over his lap, laughing as he gave me a couple of hard spanks that were just enough for me to feel it through my jeans.

"Fine, fine, but these episodes are twenty minutes long, you know. Do you think you can last that long, old man?"

His hand crashed down on my ass a few more times before he pushed me to standing.

"Quit distracting me woman!" When I just stood there watching him he added, "Take off your clothes."

"Won't that distract you more?" I sassed.

"Not as much as it will you."

We both hurried to take off our clothes, tossing things everywhere in our rush to get naked. Liam led me behind the couch, leaning me over the back.

"Keep your hands on the cushion and your eyes on the TV," he ordered in that bossy dom voice that did funny things to my insides.

He pressed a button on the remote, starting another episode. As soon as it started, he pressed up against me, his already hard cock sliding along my ass crack, and leaned over my back. His hands went to my breasts, which were swinging free beneath my body, and he gave them each a long sharp pull.

"How have we not tried nipple clamps yet?" he mused.

I turned my head to respond, and he smacked me right across my breast.

"Ow!"

"Face forward," he reminded me, returning to pinch and pull at my nipples until I was making little whining noises.

He pulled back, sliding his dick back and forth between my ass cheeks a few times. I knew he was thinking about fucking me there. I hadn't agreed to that yet, but given how much I'd liked the butt plug, I likely would soon. It's just that his cock was so much thicker than that plug...

I gasped as he shoved into my pussy in one long, hard push. I was already wet, but not as primed as I usually was, and his thick cock stretched me painfully. He landed a smack on my ass.

"Relax Coco! You're cutting off the circulation in my dick!"

I blew out a breath and as my body adjusted, Liam began pumping in and out of me in slow, shallow strokes.

In front of me, something entertaining was happening on the television, but damned if I could tell you what it was. My entire focus was tuned on my core, the sensation of Liam's slow strokes, his balls hitting my ass, his hairy legs rubbing against the back of my thighs.

And most of all, the sense of pure relief that I was back with the man I loved.

Liam reached around again, first playing with my nipples, then playing with my clit, teasing and torturing me, bringing me close to orgasm again and again, then slowing down with a reminder that I wasn't allowed to come.

By the time the final credits came on, I was a horny mess.

"Liam!" I gasped. "I need to come. Please!"

Instead of answering me, he started pounding into me at a frantic pace while I braced my hands more firmly on the seat of the couch. My breasts were swaying back and forth beneath me, and I could feel the first tremors of my orgasm building.

"Liam. I love you. Please let me come."

He stopped dead, and I groaned in frustration.

"You love me?" His voice was full of wonder. "You never said that before."

"And I'm never going to say it again if you don't fuck me into an orgasm," I snapped. "Right. Now."

I heard him chuckle behind me before grabbing my hips and resuming his hard thrusts. When he pinched my clit hard and murmured, "Come for me now, baby," I let myself go, screaming as my orgasm thundered through my body.

Liam was right behind me, his rhythm faltering as he released ropes of his milky cum inside me, filling me up with groans of pleasure.

"I love you, Coco," he whispered against my shoulder.

Another hard push, another sensation of warmth as he released more cum.

"Only you."

When he was finally done, we collapsed on the floor behind the couch, arms and legs tangled, my head on his chest.

"You made it twenty minutes," he reminded me. "Now you get a special treat."

I lifted my head and pressed a soft kiss on his lips. "I already got a special treat. Love."

Epilogue – Six Months Later

"I get to be Maid of Honor AND Best Woman! This is the best day ever!"

My sister's smile lit up her face.

"What about the day WE got married?" her new husband asked from the front row.

She waved at him impatiently. "Yeah, yeah, that was pretty good too."

Liam gave me a smile. We'd come to Las Vegas on a double date weekend and once we got here, we told my sister that the trip was also our elopement.

People in our small town had finally stopped gossiping about how Liam was "making his way through the Leahy sisters" as if there were more of us and he was some kind of Casanova. For my part, I was the "poor girl" whose husband had died, leaving her to take her sister's castoffs.

At this point all I could do was laugh about it, but there was no way I was going to ruin my wedding day with the presence of small-town gossips. We hadn't even invited our parents, and I knew both Liam's and mine were going to be pissed about that, but we wanted this day to be just for us.

We'd waited long enough for it.

Mya would be disappointed that I hadn't invited her, but she would understand. She knew the entire complicated mess that was mine and Liam's road to forever, and the role my sister had played in helping us find each other again.

Liam and I figured we'd throw a party when we got back, that sounded way more fun than having a wedding and a reception.

After much discussion, we'd agreed that if we were going to get married in Las Vegas, we had to have an Elvis impersonator as officiant.

I was pretty sure this Elvis was drunk, but that wasn't going to deter us from getting hitched.

We said the vows, Liam kissed the bride, and then we'd gone out for an extravagant celebration dinner with my sister and new brother-in-law. He was a great guy, perfect for my sister, and Liam and I both liked him.

Now we were holed up in our hotel room, stuffed from our enormous dinner, and debating whether we should have sex.

"It's our wedding night, aren't we contractually obligated to have sex or something?" I asked.

Liam groaned, rubbing his full belly. "How about you hop on and ride my cock and I can just lay here."

"No way, I'm not doing all the work on our first time as husband and wife," I shot back.

In the end, we snuggled on the bed until we both fell asleep and when the sun rose in the morning Liam used my wedding veil to tie my hands to the headboard and he ate me out until I was crying for him to let me come.

"I should have put something in the vows about not being allowed to edge me every damn time," I grumbled afterward.

"I don't edge you every time," Liam protested. "Sometimes I spank you first."

He untied my hands, and I pushed him onto his back, sliding down his naked body until I got to his cock. I gave him a few rough strokes, squeezing a few drops of precum out of the tip.

"Hold onto the headboard," I ordered.

"You think you're in control now?"

I squeezed his dick hard enough to make his hips twitch.

"Oh, I know I am." I squeezed again. "Hands on the headboard."

Liam complied, reaching up to grab the wooden frame that was screwed into the wall.

I shifted down between his thighs, kissing along the lower ridges of his abdomen, down to his upper thighs, then back again before I finally pressed a soft kiss to the tip of his dick.

"Coco!" His voice was a warning.

I playfully tapped his cock, making it bob back and forth.

"Be a good boy and I'll give you a treat."

I lowered my head, taking just the tip of him into my mouth, sucking and swirling my tongue around him until he was jerking his hips, trying to get deeper. I rewarded him by taking him as deep as I could, lowering my head until his cock touched the back of my throat and my eyes started to water. Then I pulled back and did it again, over and over until his breathing turned harsh.

"Bend your knees and open them out to the side," I instructed.

He complied immediately and I returned to sucking him like the best kind of lollipop. When I knew he was getting close, I pulled off him with a pop, sucking my finger into my mouth.

Before he knew what I was doing, I lowered my mouth back to his cock but slid my damp finger beneath him, rubbing it around his asshole. With my other hand I gave his balls a gentle squeeze.

Liam groaned loudly and when I hummed around his cock, he lost control, releasing his cum down my throat in long, milky ropes of wetness. I drank him down, and kept sucking him until he gave me the rest of his cum. When he was finally done, I licked him clean then draped myself across the front of his body like a human blanket.

"How did you like submitting to me?" I asked saucily.

He looked at me with glazed eyes. "I liked that way more than I would have expected."

"Oh good, maybe next time we'll try the butt plug on you then, husband."

"Don't push your luck, wife."

***

If you liked this book, please leave me a rating or review. Keep reading for a special sneak preview of my spicy romantic comedy "Spanking & Sprinkles".

Be sure to sign up for Reba's newsletter to get a free book and be the first to hear about new releases, special sales, and free offers. Join the fun and ***join my newsletter here***[1].

---

1.   *https://storyoriginapp.com/giveaways/ff4a004c-e434-11ea-9482-b3f353fcff13*

Sneak Preview

Spanking & Sprinkles
By Reba Bale

"Are you biting my ass, you kinky bastard?"

I looked over my shoulder at the tattooed hunk who was currently nibbling on the skin of my derriere. He looked up with a smile that most people would think was flirty if they didn't know Buck the way I did.

"You have a bitable ass, darlin'," he said, biting down hard to prove his point.

I yelped in pain, but the pain soon subsided, leaving behind a rush of moisture between my legs. Buck methodically bit a line up one butt cheek and down the other, soothing the bites with his tongue as he moved from spot to spot.

My hands were tied over my head, the rope looped over a pull-up bar Buck had installed in the doorway of his guest room. I pressed my naked body against the closed door, instinctively pulling away, but there was no place to go. I was trapped between the door and Buck's enormous body.

I had a feeling that I'd be remembering those bites every time I sat down tomorrow. The thought made me smile.

I'd never understood the part of me that liked a little pain – craved it even – but I wasn't about to analyze it too closely, not when I had a hot giant nibbling on my ass.

Buck slowly shifted to standing, rubbing his body against mine, his erect cock sliding between my ass cheeks.

"I'd love to fuck this ass," he whispered near my right ear, right before he bit down on the lobe, causing me to squirm.

"I don't do anal on the first date," I said primly.

He chuckled as he rolled his hips, the motion making the tip of his cock move up and down my crack. I suppressed a moan.

"That's okay, I'd prefer to wreck that tight little pussy our first time together anyway."

***

One month earlier...

"You're listening to James and Delilah, right here on KHZY FM. Now, who's looking forward to Valentine's Day?"

"Do we have to listen to this shit?" I hissed to my best friend and employee Lisa.

She looked up from the tray of cupcakes she was decorating and gave me a big smile.

"You may have noticed there's not a lot of radio options here in Hazy Cove. Maybe you forgot while you were gone living your glamorous life in the big city."

"Technically, Portland's a small city," I corrected, shaking a bottle of sprinkles over my own tray of cupcakes with a little too much vehemence.

I'd forgotten a lot of things about this small town on the Oregon coast while I'd been away living in Portland for so many years, including the way everyone in town was obsessed with holidays.

It didn't matter what holiday. Christmas, Valentine's Day, Flag Day, the citizens of Hazy Cove celebrated them all. Most of the time I didn't mind, but all the hoopla over Valentine's Day was really getting on my nerves. Everywhere I looked in town it was all big red hearts and cupids and love. I shuddered. It was still January for cripe's sake.

My mother would say I was only cranky about it because I didn't have a Valentine. My mother had always been way more romantic than I was, which was funny for a woman who'd gotten knocked up by her married boyfriend and then abandoned to raise her child all on her own.

I grabbed my tray of cupcakes and pasted on the sweet smile that residents expected from their local purveyor of cupcakes, heading out into the main shop area. After all, I had an image to maintain.

Culver's Cupcakes, known by the locals simply as 'the Cupcake Shop', was a Hazy Cove institution. My grandmother had started a bakery specializing in cupcakes before I was even born. She'd passed on the shop – and her secret recipes—to my mother, and my mother to me.

Like Mom, I'd grown up here making cupcakes, but I'd always had bigger dreams. I didn't want to spend my life making cupcakes for tourists and nosy locals, I wanted to move to Portland and make something of myself in the city.

And I had.

After getting my master's in business administration at Portland State University I'd been snatched up by a local consultant company, providing technical assistance to small and medium sized businesses around the Pacific Northwest. In Portland I spent my days wearing heels and power dresses and analyzing spreadsheets and business plans. I spent my nights eating in fancy restaurants and dating rich guys in suits.

Then Mom got sick, and suddenly money and the glamorous life felt less important. Mom was the only family I had, there was no way I'd leave her alone while she went through chemo.

Six months ago, I'd taken a leave of absence from my job and come home to Hazy Cove to take care of my mother and the family cupcake shop. I traded power suits for cupcake themed dresses and put on the persona of the sweet and cheerful baker instead of a hardened business expert.

I'd planned to just keep things afloat until Mom got better and could return to baking. She was feeling much better, and thank God for that, but now she was making noises about retiring and passing the cupcake shop onto me. And for some reason, I didn't hate the idea anymore.

I was going to need to make a decision sooner or later – go back to my high-powered job and my fancy condo in the Pearl District or pack up my stuff and move back here and spend the rest of my life quietly making cupcakes.

Honestly, I still wasn't sure what I was going to pick.

I glanced out the window at the waves crashing against the rocks, a grey haze making the beach look almost spooky. The scene made me smile. This part of the Pacific coast was rarely warm, but the wind whipping across the rocky coast line called to me. It felt like home in a way Portland never had.

Grabbing the coffee pot from behind the counter, I wandered around from table to table filling up cups and chatting with the customers. Daisy and Wanda were huddled in the corner, looking at something on an iPad. The two older ladies were childhood friends who were somehow still getting into trouble long past the age where most people were sitting at home in their rockers.

Daisy looked like a sweet little old lady in her red velour sweatsuit, but I knew for a fact she was inked up from top to bottom and had been quite a hell-raiser in her youth. My grandmother had always talked about her in hushed tones, sharing stories of Daisy's wild days before she married Don, opened a tattoo shop, and started a family.

"How are you ladies doing today?" I asked politely. "More coffee?"

I looked up to see Daisy watching me with an appraising look on her face.

"She'll do, don't you think?" she asked her friend.

Wanda looked me up and down. "She's perfect. She's pretty and sturdy."

Oh my God, were these old ladies calling me fat? Sure, I was curvier than a lot of women, but I kept in good shape and dressed in a way that highlighted my figure. Well, back in Portland I did anyway. I was a little more lax about my appearance here, and honestly it was possible I'd been sampling our cupcakes a little too much. I resolved to do some Pilates tonight.

"Maddie dear, we need a favor."

I felt a sense of trepidation. "What kind of a favor?"

"I need you to try to win my grandson."

*

For more of the story, check out "Spanking & Sprinkles[1]" by Reba Bale, available for immediate download on your favorite retail sites today.

---

1. https://books2read.com/u/mBJZMR

Other Books by Reba Bale

Check out my other books, available on most major online retailers now. Go to my webpage[1] at bit.ly/AuthorRebaBale to learn more.

The Unexpectedly Mine Erotic Romance Series
Sinful Desires
Taken by Surprise
Just One Night
Forbidden Desires
The Love is In the Air Series
Spanking & Sprinkles
Menage Romances
Pie Promises
Tornado Warning
Summer in Paradise
Life of the Mardi
Bases Loaded
Two for One Deal
Hotwife Erotic Romances
Hotwife in the Woods
Hotwife on the Beach
Hotwife Under the Tree
A Hotwife's Retreat
Hot Wife Happy Life
Friends to Lovers Lesbian Romance Series
The Divorcee's First Time
My BFF's Sister
My Rockstar Assistant

---

1. https://books2read.com/ap/nB2qJv/Reba-Bale

My College Crush
My Fake Girlfriend
My Secret Crush
My Holiday Love
My Valentine's Gift
My Spring Fling
My Forbidden Love
Coming Out in Ten Dates
Worth Waiting For
My Office Wife
My Party Planner

The Surrender Club Lesbian Romance Series

Jaded
Hated
Fated
Saved
Caged
Dared

Want a free book? Just join my newsletter here[2].
You'll be the first to hear about new releases, special sales, and free offers.

---

2. *https://storyoriginapp.com/giveaways/ff4a004c-e434-11ea-9482-b3f353fcff13*

About the Author

Reba Bale writes erotic romance, lesbian romance, menage romance, & the spicy stories you want to read on a cold winter's night. When Reba is not writing she is reading the same naughty stories she likes to write.

You can also follow me on Ream[3] for free stories, bonus epilogues, and exclusive content for subcribers. You can also hear all about new releases and special sales by joining Reba's newsletter mailing list.[4]

---

3.   https://reamstories.com/rebabale

4.   https://bit.ly/rebabooks

Don't miss out!

Visit the website below and you can sign up to receive emails whenever Reba Bale publishes a new book. There's no charge and no obligation.

https://books2read.com/r/B-A-IDTM-DJUOC

BOOKS 2 READ

Connecting independent readers to independent writers.